Toby Weston (born May ㄷ
and technologist.

His work weaves action and   ⌐aling
with the themes of conscious   ⌐opia, and the
technological singularity.

His books are grounded in science, but he is prepared to
take excursions into the fantastic.

Before writing books, Toby worked as a parking atten-
dant, spook, tour guide, software engineer and chef (if
you count making sandwiches).

His academic background spans Software Engineering,
Computational Neuroscience, Environmental Biology
and Deep Learning.

He is currently based in Switzerland where he writes and
works in the field of digital innovation.

SINGULARITY'S CHILDREN

BOOK ONE
DENIAL

By
Toby Weston

LOBSTER

Copyright

Published by
Lobster Books

Copyright © Toby Weston 2016

ISBN 978-0995515802

1.6.7

For
all my family

CONTENTS

A glossary of technologies and locations from the books and a full *dramatis personæ* of characters will be available at:

www.tobyweston.net

PREFACE

The Earth of this book is not ours;
it's a butterfly flap away.

This is not important. It is mostly a literary device to allow the author lenience with dates and with histories past and future.

Mostly.

Globs of viscous sauce coiled with the current. A petite woman, in white one-piece overalls, worked her way around the pool's edge to where a paper cup and party hat floated half submerged, trapped up against a filter grating. The woman swept a fine net through the water, using its long telescopic pole to retrieve food and party detritus before it could sink.

The other teenage boys, having lost interest in the pool and its residents, had moved away to play a variation of table tennis across the mounds of uneaten food that still decorated the picnic tables.

"His mother's called Anna. She's over there in the other pen," the woman said, pointing across the pool. "She had to learn the symbols as an adult, but Blue here grew up with the interface."

Niato watched as a sequence of pictograms appeared on the screen of the large Companion lying across his knees. The woman would presumably be seeing the same symbols on the chunky pair of waterproof Spex she wore over the hood of her wetsuit.

'Blue; Anna; question'

"He wants to go back to his mother," she explained.

Niato looked away in response to an agonising cry that morphed into a snarled expletive. Ignoring his friends, he turned again to the woman in the pool.

"Just a few minutes more?" He pleaded.

"Okay. Just a couple."

'Blue; fish; question'

"Now he wants more fish," she said.

"There aren't any," Niato said, shaking the empty bucket.

"Send him 'Fish' and 'Empty.'"

"Wouldn't that mean the fish is empty?"

"No, the grammar is simplified. Actually, 'Empty' stands in for any 'Negative'. It can mean 'no' or 'nothing.'"

Niato pecked at the matrix of symbols covering most of the Companion's screen—a grid of picture icons displaying a few dozen nouns and verbs. He chose symbols and strung together a sentence for the young dolphin.

'Fish; empty'

To soften the blow, Niato also sent:

'Boy; loves; Blue'

Blue lifted his face out of the water and peered sideways at Niato. He wore a skull cap that housed the neural scanning hardware, enabling their crude cross-species conversation. It was held in place by a tube of neoprene; it looked just like a black balaclava with Blue's smiling beak poking comically out of the front.

had hardly scratched its surface. There had been so many questions he would have asked that were too clumsy and cryptic to formulate with the handful of symbols at his disposal. He had felt cheated. For a long time, he could not understand the point of hobbling their communication.

The limitation wasn't with the dolphin's capacity for learning. Blue was named explicitly in papers where researchers explored complex abstract concepts. He was a prodigy. The language might not be his mother tongue, but it was close. He had been communicating with the pictograms since he was a calf.

'Fish; fish; fish; moon; fish; fish; fish; moon; clock; empty'

Blue would have known the moon. Swimming cramped laps within the tiled artificial rectangle, it would have been one of the few intrusions of a wider organic world.

Awareness of privilege had begun eroding Niato's sense of worth. He needed a purpose. He decided he needed to talk with this friend again.

It had not been easy to get access to the Institute's computers, but he was a capable teenager with access to considerable resources. Even so, his first attempt at recruiting a Cyber-Ronin had ended with a scammer disappearing with all of his CryptoCoins. As a silver lining, the pity generated had transmuted via emotional alchemy into reputation, and he had made contact with a group of genuine hacktivists.

These new friends provided the means. At first, they had wanted to sell him their standard ransom-ware and cyber-griefing packages, but he wanted something more elegant. He wanted to talk to Blue and let him know he understood the crime. The Institute was keeping Blue physically captive; but, even worse, having given him the capacity to communicate, they were denying him the opportunity.

'Fish; fish; fish; moon; fish; fish; fish; moon; fish; fish; fish; moon; clock; empty'.

Days spent eating stiff, still fish. Tedium measured by the cycles of the moon. A life of repetition and monotony and at the end, when his time was over, nothing, empty.

The network penetration had been elegant: a remote, un-audited tunnel between Blue's interface and Niato's Companion. Illicit nights spent in secret communication had followed. The link between the two adolescent mammals became a joining of worlds.

Linguistic gag gone, Blue used his voice, at first, to rail furiously against his captors, with Niato lumped in alongside every other human. He was angry. Niato took long, patient weeks to establish some level of credibility; but slowly, as he explained in simple crude brush strokes the world outside the Institute, Blue had calmed down, hot anger transitioning into cold resolution.

They left childhood together. Their world views merged. Blue, in his pool, wanted to smash it all. Niato, with freedom to operate, felt obligated to assist.

'Big; ocean; dirty; question' Blue asked one day.

'Boy; clean; ocean' Niato replied, pecking out his response.

Over the next few years, newspapers gleefully reported Niato's acts of sabotage and vandalism, delighting in the shame the Munisai clan's eldest son was bringing down on his family. His father, never hands-on, had tried clumsily to correct his son's wayward course, but Niato had become an embarrassment and, eventually, at his grandfather's insistence, he had been cast out.

As far as the family was concerned, he had been radicalised and recruited.

*****

'Blue; clock; ocean; question'

'Today; night; four; clock' Niato selected the symbols on the surface of his Companion. The room was full of the sounds and smells of sleeping terrorists.

Blue didn't send a response but Niato, could imagine he would be whistling loudly in his pool, excitement making him fall back to native sounds.

Some of the others were now groaning and stretching as Companion alarms vibrated.

'Goodbye;'
'Boy; love; Blue' Niato sent, feeling a little self-conscious.

'Today; night; ocean' Blue sent back.

Niato struggled out of his sleeping bag. It was six o'clock in the afternoon, but their direct-action-collective had been running on an adjusted cycle in preparation for tonight's action and it felt like the middle of the night. Light from the dropping sun shone through slots in the blackout blinds. Somebody was making coffee. The smell made its way into the room and had the desired effect of accelerating the waking process.

Niato called up the Nebulous, the protest vessel lurking sixty miles offshore. He checked in with the two-man crew, who would stick around the newly freed dolphins for the first few days. Everything was ready. They had plenty of fish in reserve in case Blue or his mother were unable to hunt. They would soon start motoring towards the rendezvous.

Niato pulled his jacket over his fleece and slung the back-pack over his shoulder. It was cold outside as they waited for Jack in the collective's knackered old hatchback. A few other people were around. An elderly woman with shopping bags passed by and eyed the huddle of youths suspiciously.

Eventually, a car rattled to a halt and they piled in, stuffing all their gear in the back. The driver turned around and did a quick head count, then pulled away. At thirty-five, Jack was the old man.

Niato sat up front. In the back, Dee and Shota were squashed up against the windows by Yuto's expansive butt. The car now contained a third of the eco-collective; the others should be on their way too, riding in other vehicles. The reputation and allure of an eco-insurgency run by a dolphin and the wayward son of a billionaire attracted a steady flow of new members; all but the most hard-core were turned away.

This would be the group's second prison-break operation. A bold step up from the previous target, which had been a sea park conveniently located on the coast. A quick snip with the bolt croppers had opened a gate, and their marine comrades had swum into an estuary and then out to sea and freedom. Unfortunately, the Institute of Mammalian Cognition was twenty-five kilometres inland.

Niato glanced at Dee in the mirror. She was probably two years younger than he was, sixteen or seventeen, he guessed, dressed like the others in black.

'Boy; clock; question' Blue sent.

'One; clock' Niato replied.

He nodded to the driver of the white van as they passed it on the freeway. By design, all the vehicles were older models requiring manual control. Automation might shirk at some manoeuvres they would be forced to make over the next couple of hours.

The last time he had visited the Institute in person had been nearly four years ago. It wasn't a tourist attraction. It had only been the influence and generous donations of Niato's family that had ever persuaded them to host a spoilt teenager's birthday party in the first place.

The Institute was set in its own grounds, encircled by scrubby forest. Faint simian hoots echoed over the high, functional walls surrounding and obscuring the buildings within. They kept to the trees until they received a message, suggesting the cameras and alarms might now be offline. The sender had made sure to employ enough conditionals and weasel words in his message that he would be absolved of all responsibility in any event.

Dee, boosted by Yuto, swung a wad of blankets over the glass shards embedded into the top of the wall. She tested with her hands; then, using Yuto's shoulders and head as a ladder, climbed over and dropped quietly down the other side. Niato followed in the same fashion, apologising as he abused his friend's face with his toe.

A riot of screams and a metallic beating of cages erupted from within a low building to their left. Lights tripped by movement flicked on. They froze, holding their breath as they waited for alarms, but apparently the circuits were all local.

With a pang of guilt, Niato ignored the primates and they pressed on to the pool, where Blue and his mother and sister would be waiting.

'Boy;pool' he sent, then grinned as he heard his friend's excited chittering. Emotion modulated compression waves in air; direct and ancient.

'Light; man; where; question' Niato asked.

A few seconds later, a map appeared on Niato's Companion, showing him Blue's best guess at the position of the night watch. The neural interface allowed Blue to choose pictograms by mentally bumping a virtual pallet, in the same way he could indicate locations on the map of the Institute Niato had uploaded.

Perfect; the man was still in the hut by the front gate. Dee turned to Niato and they exchanged raised eyebrows. He nodded towards the back gate and she headed off. He continued on towards the fence around the dolphin pool. He used pliers to cut through the wire mesh and, making sure the gap was wide enough, used cable ties to fold the fence back out of the way. The lights were still off inside the dolphin compound, but he could make out shapes in the water surging towards the soft sounds of his feet.

Another combustion engine arrived. He heard talking, then several loud clicks as bolt croppers were used to 'unlock' the back delivery gate.

'Light; man;' Blue sent with a new map, showing the security guard was on the move.

The monkeys had calmed down, and the place was quiet again. Niato crouched down against a low wall. He could see the beam of a torch swaying from side to side as the guard did his rounds.

Now came the tricky part.

From the front came a commotion. The decoy drunken and injured hikers had arrived. Niato could hear shouting and a booming, as fists beat on the front gate. The torch halted mid-swing. At the next boom, the guard turned and headed off back towards the reception at the front of the Institute. Niato could just make out his irritated muttering.

In a crouching scuttle, Niato covered the few metres to the side of the pool.

'Quiet' he sent, trying to calm the excited whistles. The three dolphins had lifted their chests out of the water and were sculling in tight circles, craning to resolve Niato's shape.

Silently, Dee led six new arrivals to where Niato was crouching at the water's edge.

"Who first?" she asked.

'Go; Blue; Anna; Tinkerbell; question' Niato sent.

The dolphins dropped back below the surface. Niato's Companion tried to decipher the dialog passing between them, but little seemed to be in the Institute's language.

After what seemed like several minutes, Dee looked significantly at Niato. Time was critical; they needed to load three dolphins into two vans and bugger off before the drunk, injured, and confused hiker act wore thin and the guard came back to check for whatever had spooked the rhesus monkeys.

'Clock' he sent.

Seconds later, Blue surfaced and looked sideways at Niato.

'Anna;Tinkerbell' Blue sent.

"Let's start with the mother, then the baby," Niato said to the other humans.

Dee and Shota slipped into the water with the larger sling. Niato joined them and swam out to cajole Anna into the shallows. Initially, she was compliant; but proximity to—and then contact with—the sling made her increasingly agitated. Suddenly, with a colossal splash, she surged away.

"Shit. Looks like mother has some trauma from when she was captured," Shota said.

"Okay, let's try Tinkerbell then. Let me tell Blue the change of plan," Niato said.

'Tinkerbell' he sent to Blue.

Blue seemed to understand and nudged his sister towards the smaller sling. The baby swam past, nervously keeping close to its mother, who had returned from a ragged circuit of the pool. For the first time, Niato noticed the white scarring across the baby's brow and the slight bulge between her eyes. He had read about the operation, but still recoiled at the sight.

At the last minute, the little dolphin seemed to notice it was being lifted out of the water and began to flex and whistle with panic. This set off another uncomfortable episode from Anna. Blue swam to his splashing, screaming mother; he nuzzled her and thrummed calming vibrations through the water between them.

Now, the baby was out of the water on her way to the van. She was small enough that just two people were able to carry her through the gap in the fence Niato had cut.

The others, still at the pool, tried again with the mother; Niato stroking her back, while Blue lay against her side. They moved her again over the sling. She was clearly agitated, but the sight and sounds of her baby being carried away out of the water and beyond her reach seemed to galvanise her resolve, and she permitted the sides of the canvas sling to be raised up. It took four pole-bearers to lift her out of the water.

Everybody was concentrating now, focusing on the tricky operation and trying not to slip or drop the awkward, flexing, 400-kilogram tube. Nobody noticed a new arrival.

"What the hell is this?" asked the astonished voice of the security guard. He had rounded the wall and was staring incredulously at the pantomime playing out on the other side of the pool.

The rescuers froze, petrified, mid-pose. The guard fumbled at his hip.

The brief awkward stand-off persisted until Blue's cackling urged them to action. Yuto gave the pole a push, and the others clambered out of the water and started to hurry off in the direction of the truck.

"Hey!" the guard shouted. He equivocated for another two seconds, then shot at the largest available target. The electro-dart arced sub-sonically over the water. Yuto grunted and staggered as it penetrated his gluteus. Without his support, the sling sagged and the others strained to keep the mother from rolling out onto the wet tiles.

Niato tried not to betray any signs of awareness as he picked out the shape of their colleague—the male half of the drunken hiker distraction—creeping up behind the guard; but, alerted by a sound, the guard turned at the last second and, without fuss, shot the miraculously sober hiker point blank. His would-be attacker fell, writhing, to the ground.

Back in the van, the baby Tinkerbell had begun a screaming lament. Anna answered with her own high, dry whistle and flexed her tail in panic. Three sets of straining arms endeavoured to keep control.

The guard had approached the pool and faced the group across eight metres of agitated water.

'Anna; Tinkerbell; ocean' Blue sent. Niato could make out his form at the bottom of the pool, approaching quickly.

"No!" he shouted, understanding his friend's plan.

A bulb of water bulged and burst.

The shocked guard staggered back from the edge, but not fast enough to avoid the mouth that closed on his extended forearm. Inertia lifted him off his feet and then gravity tugged them both back into the pool.

The water closed over. Ripples stilled. A stunned silence descended.

"Get them to the fucking van!" Jack shouted, breaking the spell.

Yuto had pulled out the dart.

Limping heavily, they set off to where Tinkerbell was still keening pitifully.

"He's called backup. We couldn't stop him!" shouted Tori, the other drunken hiker, now also arriving on the scene.

She crouched down to help her friend, who was slowly regaining control after his electric shocking.

With a splash, the guard cleared the surface, coughing and thrashing his arms. Before he could take more than a lungful of air, he was tugged down again by the teeth, now fixed on his ankle. Sirens could be heard in the distance.

"Oh shit, it's going to kill him!" Jack screamed.

'Stop' Niato sent.

'Light; man; stay'
'Boy; go' Blue sent back.

"Go!" Dee shouted. "I'll stay and sort this out. They won't be able to hold me."

"She's right. She's a juvenile. The police won't be able to touch her. Let's fucking go, man!" Jack explained, somewhat hysterically.

Niato stood frozen, listening, as tyres skidded to a halt on the gravel at the front of the Institute. He didn't want to leave Blue or Dee, but he couldn't think of alternatives that didn't involve murder.

'Go' Blue sent again, allowing the thrashing guard another gasp of air.

An infinite succession of tiny wavelets slapped the canoe's wooden hull. Each an embodiment of platonic perfection, brittle and crystalline, cast from sunlight and water. As the waves met the mundane matter of the boat's hull, they shattered, their Bezier-curve beauty dissolving into a pixelated jumble of sound and light.

The girl, focusing beyond the surface chaos, pointed and giggled at the pale, shimmering ghost making its way under the boat. Marcel's white buttocks were a clear flag; the remainder of the boy's form was lost beneath a confusing mirror of reflections. Stella's mother sat at the other end of the boat, Marcel's dad resting his head on her lap. She showed uncharacteristic tenderness as she played with his hair, sometimes bending down to whisper close to his ear.

Four hundred metres away, a green bump, topped by a rocky pyramid, was surrounded by concentric halos of white and turquoise. Their boat was floating above a protrusion of reef rising close to the surface. Small fish, nosing into the nooks and crevices of the reef, fought the slow push and pull of the swell. The tide's gentle current held the anchor line taut. In front of them, towards the small island, the water deepened and then dropped to ninety metres, before rising up in a low, sandy slope to the shore. Sometimes, huge shoals of fish would be forced between the caldera's outer reef and the shore as they chased seething balls of baitfish. On lucky days, Marcel's village would catch them and celebrate.

Stella pulled on her flippers, glanced one more time at her mother, and plopped into the scintillating waters. She swam towards Marcel, who was now using his folded arms to hang off the outrigger. He smiled, still breathing hard from his dive. She couldn't emulate Marcel's effortless grace, but, with a splash and some floundering at the surface, she dived and paddled down with her feet, her arms at her sides. A stream of bubbles rose from the corners of her mouth and floated chaotically toward the surface. She came up next to her friend.

She had been thinking about grabbing his feet as she surfaced; but, ultimately afraid, unable to gauge his response, she had changed her mind. They had only been friends for a few hours, since the boy's father had picked them up from the Farm and sailed them here to his ancestral island. The boy and his father spoke only a little English and Cantonese. Stella was able to piece together conversations in Nipponese or Alman, and she knew bits and pieces, or could at least recognise, half a dozen more languages spoken by the fishermen and crew in this part of the world. Even so, the narrow linguistic overlap with the island's patois left the two children communicating mostly at the level of gestures and smiles.

The boy grinned at her as she grabbed onto the outrigger. Stella looked at her mom. She was still smiling, eyes closed. Stella had never seen her mother in such a good mood for such a long period of time—unless she was high. But those times didn't count because, as soon as she was not high, she'd drop into a murderous rage. By the age of six, Stella had known how things worked, and she tried not to be around at those times. Perhaps, her mother was high now. Stella had noticed none of the nasty equipment, but maybe she'd smoked something while Stella hadn't been watching. Perhaps, that was why the boy was out here.

Perhaps, he was waiting as far away as he could get for the inevitable rage.

"You scared of your dad?" she asked, while engaging the appropriate gestures and mimes in case he didn't understand.

"Scared?" he repeated the unfamiliar word.

Stella clutched her hands to her sternum and mimed a frightened face, complete with quivering lip. "Scared, afraid, you understand?"

"Yes, understand. No fear."

"Why are you trying to get away from them? Scared of my mom? No problem, she never hits other children."

"Huh? Hit your mother? Only swimming." He thought for a few seconds, unsettled by the strange questions. "Your Mom, she… hitting?" he asked, demonstrating a hand slapping his face.

Stella didn't answer, suddenly afraid her mother might have been watching their pantomimes of violent domestic dysfunction. There didn't seem to be a logical progression from this point, so Marcel dived down below the surface again with his little spear gun. Stella dipped her head to follow his progress.

The island was part of a marine park controlled by the Nipponese/Prussian conglomerate that ran the huge floating farms. Marcel's father was considered lucky by the islanders; he had managed to get a job on a farm, the same one where Stella and her mother lived. He still kept a hut where his first wife and other children lived. Stella, having grown up on the cramped, hectic Farm, thought this island looked much nicer; at least you could climb up the hill if a big storm came.

She watched Marcel swim gently up to a parrotfish and shoot it expertly through the gills, from about a metre away. The fish thrashed in a futile attempt to escape the metal rod that had pierced its head, its life tinting the water red. Then Marcel swam up, breaking the surface with his raised hand, triumphantly clutching the speared fish. The grown-ups, looking over at the commotion, clapped and waved their congratulations to him.

"I try?" Stella asked, as the boy took the still struggling fish off the spear and dropped it into the canoe.

"Yes, you know how gun work?"

She nodded. The boy leant on the spear gun, pressing the point of the bolt against the tough old wood of the outrigger. It slipped deeper into the barrel, until there was a click.

"Fish, then trigger." He repeated the motions for Stella. "Be close to fish. Okay?"

Stella nodded and accepted the barrel; it was heavier than she had expected. She grinned at the boy and then pushed herself down into the water with her free hand. Marcel ducked beneath the surface too, pressing his hands against the underside of the boat to keep himself submerged as he watched.

Stella found it difficult to swim with just one arm, but she pumped her flippers hard enough to send herself down toward a shoal of silver fish, drifting with the waves near a big outcrop of coral. She was running out of breath and her ears were hurting, so she gave one last paddle, held the gun out in front, and squeezed the trigger.

The spear left a trail of bubbles as it shot out toward the shoal; but, by the time it reached the fish, it was travelling slowly enough that, with a minimum of fuss, the school flicked out of its way. Disappointed, but somehow relieved that she hadn't hurt anything, Stella kicked her legs and let herself float back up to the surface. Marcel gathered the loops of barely visible line and fitted the spear back into the gun. He insisted she take it and have another go.

By the time she finally got one, the sun was almost down. Flushed with success, Stella swam over to the boat to show her mom the prize. She could see Marcel's father leaning back with his eyes closed, but she wanted her own mother to see the fish. She pulled herself out of the water and brought her eyes level with the side of the canoe, but she had already inadvertently sent a surge of water onto Marcel's father's lap and, unexpectedly, onto the back of her mother's head.

Electrocuted by the cold water, her mother turned and screamed "Sei hoi! I'm busy!"

Stella dropped back into the water. She forgot about the fish, which swam away trailing a bloody mist. Marcel followed, eventually scooping it up with a net once it had exhausted itself, and brought it back to her.

"You okay? Why she angry?"

"She's busy."

Much later, they grilled the fish on a flat stone, in the middle of the canoe, while the grown-ups drank little cups of wine. Marcel cooked Stella's fish and prepared it on a banana leaf for her. Stella's mom jeered at this, pointing at the kids and whispering something to Marcel's dad. He didn't look like he thought whatever she said was very funny. Stella wondered why her mom said nasty things. She could already tell that Marcel's dad was getting tired of her; couldn't her mom see it, too?

They slept on the boat that night. It got cold once dusk descended and the disappearing sun left a chill. Marcel and Stella slept next to each other in their sleeping bags. Marcel's father had covered them with a tarpaulin to stop the dew soaking them through.

Sometime in the night, the inevitable argument came. After the children had fallen asleep, Stella's mom insisted on smoking a little pipe before bed. Marcel's dad raised his voice in protest, and her mom shrieked back at him like a harpy. Stella, attuned to the dangers her mother presented, flicked her eyes open in time to watch the man's face. In the firelight, she saw rage, resignation, and then indifference follow one another in quick succession. She closed her eyes. She knew they wouldn't be coming here again.

The BHJ HR minion had provided him with a flat, flat-pack box. The security guard had stood there watching disinterestedly as Anosh performed the origami necessary to extrude it into three dimensions. The guard was not necessary; Anosh wasn't going to make a fuss.

Ironic mug; pseudo-leather organiser; stapler—technically not his, but he was not challenged, enforcing property rights on stationary was not in the guard's remit—post-it notes; Bluetooth keyboard and mouse. He packed them all under the sanctimonious gaze of his former colleagues. His, or rather the company's, laptop was buzzing away on the windowsill as it erased its hard drive.

He looked at the row of technical books sharing his window alcove with the clicking drive. They had rested unmolested for years, fossils from a time when people still purchased their words on paper. Most of the technologies had enjoyed their time at the top of the hype curve and were now as obsolete as tallow candles or human compassion. Running a finger across the patiently accumulated dust, he shrugged, then dropped the bundles of cellulose into the waiting bin to join his other unwanted effects. At the last second, he reached back to retrieve a book he had been given at a recent conference—'The Four Phases of Change: Denial, Disruption, Conflict and Reimagination'. The world was changing; he would need all the help he could get.

"I heard the news, really sorry to hear you have to leave."

"Oh, yeah. Thanks," Anosh said, looking up from the book's back cover to see his colleague, Christian, hovering uncomfortably nearby.

"Seems a bit harsh if you ask me," Christian offered quietly, his eyes regularly sweeping the floor. "Can't see how the mess with Field-Goal has anything to do with you really."

Anosh didn't have the energy for this conversation, but Christian had at least made the effort to talk to the day's pariah.

"Field-Goal was basically screwed from before I took it over. There was no way we were going to be able to implement half the regulations the board had agreed to. I was just in the wrong place at the wrong time, I guess."

"What did they get you for?"

"Trying to do my job!" Anosh dug through the clutter and passed Christian the termination letter that had been waiting on his desk when he had arrived in the morning. The security guard coughed significantly. Anosh ignored him.

"Policy violation," he explained as Christian was reading. "We didn't follow the testing processes properly."

"Okay, well I suppose you really do need to follow those policies, right?" said Christian.

Anosh felt himself getting angry. He snatched back a Linux penguin snow globe the guard had picked up from his desk.

"It would have been OK if there had been a test environment to use in the first place!"

Christian glanced nervously around again. Policy violations were black and white, and he remembered the three compliancy Web Based Trainings he still had to do before the end of the month.

"Sorry to hear the news. Look, I'm sure you will land on your feet," he smiled awkwardly. "Anyway, I've got some things I have to be getting on with. See you around. It's a small world, right?"

"Yeah, bye Christian."

Socks; squash shoes; umbrella…

Once he had gathered his meagre possessions, Anosh grabbed the box and ran the gauntlet of desks towards the elevator. People stood awkwardly as he passed. With genuine or feigned concern, they extended hands. At each desk, he repeated the awkward shuffle, shifting the box onto one arm, then hooking it with his elbow to free a hand for shaking. Each time, the guard stopped with an exasperated sigh.

Poor guy, thought Anosh, he probably had a half-dozen other people to escort out of the building this morning. Anosh took the long route through the cubicles to avoid his boss's glass-walled office. He didn't want to be exposed to her vapid sympathy; he wasn't sure he could remain calm in the face of her impeccably faked emotions. She always left him feeling livid, yet somehow simultaneously guilty for the emotional anguish he was causing her. It was as if he was a problem child incapable of even the most basic tasks.

She had done well. A few years previously, when the company had merged with BHJ, she had stepped in as project manager. In her version of reality, she had managed to turn things around and get the product out the door, despite Anosh and his team's bungles and mix-ups. After that, she had been promoted to become Anosh's line manager. Since then, she had 'managed up the chain' relentlessly, taking credit for every success, manufacturing the impression she was a miracle worker who, against the odds, was the only thing protecting the tech team from their own reckless incompetence.

With the trial of polite inane handshaking behind him, the elevator ride was a relief, despite the lurking presence of the uniformed symbol of corporate malice.

The final door revolved, spat him onto the street, and that was it. Five years, four Christmas parties, three successful projects, two awards for outstanding commitment, and one dismissal for violating policies.

It was raining. Buses, taxis, and a few cars splashed along the drenched road, their wheels creating clouds of clinging spray and flinging oily drops across the pavement. The guard stood inside, watching, just in case Anosh wanted to make a scene. He didn't.

No more corporate taxis. Trains were running today, but judging by the length of the queue to get onto the platform and the level of annoyed muttering, the service was far from optimal. He gave up and took a succession of buses that eventually dropped him a wet twenty-minute walk from his home.

When it finally came, the global *econopocalypse* had been quick, if not entirely painless. For years, the governments of the developed world had been raising taxes, mostly through inflation, on the fortunate few who still had work. It was clear to everyone, politicians included, that this was a suicidal course of action, but they didn't have an alternative. Nobody was willing to accept publicly the obvious: When factories could work without people, and vehicles could drive themselves, there were simply not enough jobs to go around.

Economists continued to sing their old songs of stimulus and counter-cyclic investment; however, by the time the majority accepted there might be a problem, it was far too late for traditional economic remedies.

Despite tradition, culture, and social conditioning, it was suddenly clear that working had become counterproductive; having much too much would never be an option, so it was better to have nothing. At least *nothing* couldn't be arbitrarily taken away.

Consumption dried up and the inevitable recession put still more people out of work. Governments printed money to pay off the unproductive masses of unemployed. Inflation, followed by hyper-inflation, pushed currencies to collapse.

Ayşe was vacuuming when he opened the door to their split-level apartment. She craned around the banister when she heard the door. Seeing him clutching the pathetic, shameful box of his work trinkets, she knew instantly.

"Oh no!" She kicked the off switch and came down the stairs to hug him awkwardly around the cardboard box he was still holding.

"It's okay." He tried to keep his voice level. "We knew this would happen, right?"

"Oh no, I was sure they would let you off. You've done so much for that damn company!"

"Please, not now. Let me just dump this and sit down."

"Okay, let me make you a tea. The boys are watching something in the play room. Why don't you go into the lounge and sit down?" Ayşe fussed, taking the damp box from him to put it down.

He tried to sneak past the door to the kids' room, but they caught him and hurtled at his legs.

"Daddy why are you home? Come and watch, Baqi is trapped and Fattah doesn't know where he is…"

"Hello there, my two little lion cubs! What are you watching?"

They scooted over and made room for him on the sofa and he kissed their heads.

Two months' pay and a further six months' unemployment before the family would be destitute. They had talked about this endlessly. Ayşe had lost her job four months ago. Even before then, they had known it was just a matter of time. The finance sections of the news were full of speculation about the next recession, although to most people it felt like they had been in a recession for the past decade. Jobs were disappearing as they were sucked up by Cloud Algorithms or split into tasks and reverse auctioned to the lowest bidder.

Neither Anosh nor Ayşe had made it into the rarefied upper echelons, and nothing else seemed safe anymore. Anosh had survived by carving out a niche for himself as a 'go to' guy, able to deliver. Each round of cost cutting had scrutinised him and ultimately, grudgingly, decided he was worth keeping. Each new manager had clarified to him he was very lucky; most roles were already outsourced, off-shored, downgraded, or terminated. On sufferance, they had allowed him to continue bringing in revenue, customers, upgrades, and features.

Ayşe brought in the stainless steel teapots and poured Anosh a glass; she had already put two small hemispherical biscuits on the side of his saucer. He lifted two tiny spoons of sugar into the amber tea and watched some young woman in a burqa crack open a prison cell with what looked like the power of prayer.

"What are they watching?"

"Boys, why did you turn off Mystery Park?"

"It finished, Mummy, and this came on. But it's okay, there's no hitting."

Two boys, just six and eight. It was crushing. Anosh knew they were lucky; they still had a reserve. Many of their friends had lost their houses and all the equity tied up in them by not reacting quickly enough to their new situation.

They had tried to maintain an extinct lifestyle with savings and credit, long after the corporate teat was removed. Anosh and Ayşe had already decided they would not let that happen. The boys would probably be too young to remember they had once lived in a nice house before Mummy and Daddy lost their jobs, and they all got poor.

The sound of super hero combat competed with the clinking of metal spoons and glass, but Anosh's mind was elsewhere. As unemployment continued to climb—by 2022, it was at twenty-nine per cent—consumers, the engine of a hundred years of capitalist expansion, had stopped consuming. Government inflation figures were stuck at one or two per cent, but they conveniently left out food, shelter, and energy. Electronics were cheap, food and fuel extortionate. The top one per cent controlled ninety per cent of the wealth and paid virtually no taxes. They squatted in their Kensington mega-basements or perched in their penthouses and stared down their host governments with petulant threats to leave every time anybody politely mentioned that, perhaps, if it was okay with them, it might be a good idea to increase taxes for the rich, maybe.

"Damn!"

The boys jumped and looked up to see why Daddy was cross again. Satisfied they were not the cause, they were quickly sucked back into their cartoon.

"We better start looking for a new place to live tomorrow," said Anosh. "I have a feeling this time it might be a while before one of us is working again."

"Okay boys," said Ayşe. "Clean your teeth and get ready

for bed."

"Oh, Mama!"

"Go on Zaki, be a good boy, and please help your brother find some pyjamas."

Grumbling for a few seconds, until they were lost in their next game, the kids hurtled out.

Anosh flicked the channel to GNN to see what the helmsmen of their stricken vessels were saying today. A chirpy Australian anchor was interviewing the British Finance Minister, while the head of the UK Forward Party sat across from him listening sceptically and waiting his turn to speak. Anosh was bored with the rhetoric and only bothered to catch snippets of what was being said.

"Easing unemployment is the prime agenda item for this government."

"The Russ are indulging in the worst kind of international oppression."

"It is disingenuous to claim that this is anything other than posturing."

"Britain has loan agreements with the IMF and ECB that guarantee our ability to pay for the gas…"

He switched it off and threw the remote into the cushions. He had long ago realised it was a sham. The political process was so profligate, polarised and partisan that, regardless of any initial altruistic motives, the players became hard-boiled politicos—willing puppets ready to accommodate any agenda offered by their hidden patrons, in exchange for their continuity of power.

The relentless grind erased all original patterns, leaving only artefacts. These husks, robbed of creativity and human empathy, were utterly incapable of steering the world out of its desperate, seemingly endless, run of bubbles and crashes.

"We have to find a new place, honey. We can't afford another day of this bloody rent!"

"Hey, the kids are still up! Please!"

Anosh looked guiltily at the two boys standing in the doorway, sucking lethargically at their toothbrushes while watching him.

"Clean your teeth. Don't just suck off the toothpaste!" Ayşe scolded, sending them off to the bathroom.

"Start looking again tomorrow," she said turning back to Anosh. "But don't worry, you will find a new job. Geißler told me Bernd just found a new one, so it can't be too bad!"

Anosh managed a smile. He supposed if the skill-less, born to middle management Trevor could find work, it really shouldn't be that tough—but it seemed Trevor had taken the last job in Prussia. In desperation, Anosh had even looked back across the Channel, but things were no better there.

They spent six months looking for a new place to live.

Competition at the bottom had perversely pushed prices

up. Ayşe refused to live in a *squalid little hole* somewhere horrible, and Anosh had rejected anything that wasn't cheaper than the luxury, split-level home they were used to. Everything became desperate for them as they saw their savings sublimate away.

When an ex-colleague in financial troubles of his own mentioned he was selling off an old family office building, they decided to go for it. Some friends had pooled resources and Anosh put in what was left of their savings. Their little collective was able to buy the old print shop building at 43 Henkelkai.

The ground floor still contained a couple of massive, dusty machines and had huge rolls of musty and decaying paper pushed to one end. For their share, Anosh and his family received the entire top floor and the roof.

Ayşe was far from thrilled to be squatting in a semi-derelict, abandoned building, but she couldn't stand firm against the onslaught of Anosh's enthusiasm for long. It would be their asylum and, eventually, he promised, their home.

The other two floors were split between three families: his old workmate, a former software test manager, and his friends, both Pakistani Sikhs. Anosh immediately hit it off with the doctor, who was called Vikram. The other guy, a former photographer who had specialised in documenting insurance claims, seemed a little stiff, but they all worked together over the first couple of weeks to clean and fix up the place for themselves and their families.

The building had probably never contained so much life. Anosh's own small litter played on the stairs or in the yard out back, with a rotating and essentially uncountable number of children; brothers and sisters, cousins and guests. In its heyday, the whole area, built on a semi-circular half island of soft mud, within a giant meander of the Rhein, had been a bustling dock with warehouses and yards. Despite a brief revival during the World War, goods sent by ship had been in decline for the past century, and the marginalised maze of locks and canals had slipped into increasing decrepitude.

The run-down, but centrally located, real-estate had been earmarked for redevelopment: old red brick buildings converted into coffee shops, design agencies, and luxury penthouse apartments. New prestigious headquarters, glass parallelograms or cylinders, surrounded by manicured grass and expensive cryptic corporate art, had been built circling the historic nucleus of restored warehouses.

Development had been sporadic. Work would stop when the markets crashed and then start again a few years later as the economy shivered and began to show signs of life. Recently, as the crashes became comically frequent, hard hats and construction sounds were predictable harbingers of the next slowdown's arrival. Many buildings were only half finished and had remained so for a decade. Ragged plastic sheeting blew from their toothless window frames. Economic refugees and other more or less legitimate inhabitants squatted in the more complete buildings.

***

Four floors up and Anosh still felt uncomfortably close to the action playing out on the streets below. The wet towel pressed to his face wasn't stopping the gas that stung his throat and nose and made his eyes weep. Ayşe was downstairs with the boys, distracting them with cartoons from a better age. Anosh wanted a first-hand look at the violence again engulfing the city. He had come up on the pretext of cleaning the snow off the panels.

They had been in the house for six months, and the electric company still hadn't reinstated the building's supply, claiming an open bill from the former tenant, so they were reduced to a reliance on the fickle whims of the sun. Periodically, Anosh would climb to the roof and manually align the panels to a bright region of clouds that might hint at the sun's location. Even on a smoky and overcast day, there was usually enough sun to boil a kettle, while slowly charging the Companion and nightlight batteries.

The main protest must have been dealt with because, from his vantage point, he could see police on horseback or in armoured vans closing in on the pathetic bunch of protestors, who were now marching raggedly along the street below. Slogans were shouted and banners waved, but there didn't seem to be much conviction left. Bells were ringing. No solemn striking of the hour or elegant cascading peals, there was no wedding to announce; the bells were for anybody who had missed the police sirens, the black smoke and the eye-watering tinge of CS gas.

Anosh stood at the railing on the roof and looked down at the stragglers, who were bringing their chaos to this normally quiet neighbourhood. They were moving through the city's outskirts with no clear target for their aggression, burning and trashing lethargically.

It was winter and it was cold. The people were angry. Many

had no jobs, no benefits, and no money. More importantly, on a freezing day like today, they had no heating. The big gas pipes from the East had been shut off again and rationing had directed what little reserves were left to hospitals, schools, and prisons. Electricity was sporadic, with blackouts most days.

Lately, either as a punishment or an encouragement to settle down, the government had started to shut off power to 'troubled' areas. It didn't seem to be working. Food and heating were scarce and the politicians seemed to have nothing left in their box of tricks; even their speeches were tired and abrupt, as if they too had finally realised no one was listening.

Shouts and cries carried along the snowy streets. More horses from a side street disorientated the huddle. In the confusion, they had allowed themselves to be tricked into taking a wrong turn. They were kettled; there was no way out, except past the massed police horses.

Looking at the concentration of meat on the hoof, a guilty thought flashed up from some primal partition of his mind and Anosh's stomach rumbled.

The riot police had formed a line and were patiently pushing back the crowds towards the banks of the canal. People were panicking as they ran out of ground. Just when Anosh thought he was about to witness a massacre, another column of protestors arrived. It was unlikely to be mere chance. The protestors had Companions, and their own mesh networks running command and control structures.

The police, who were out-manoeuvred now, found themselves sandwiched between a few hundred desperate protestors, on the brink of a plunge into the icy waters, and a fresh mass of students armed with banners, bottles, and sticks. The new arrivals were roaring with rage at what they saw unfolding before them. Some command was given and the horses turned and charged towards the new threat.

Anosh found he could connect to the protestors' mesh, and he used the opportunity to check a public view of the Battle-Space's maps, videos and tactics posts. Dusslestadt was just one battle in the war today. In Hamburg, a police station had been stormed and the city council, which had been passing emergency power laws, had been taken hostage. Fifteen protestors had already died, and it was still only early afternoon. When it got too chilly or cold on the roof and the battle became too close and real, he continued to follow it with their Companion from downstairs.

He kept the device in sleep mode to save battery, only turning it on at fifteen-minute intervals or when a roar from outside signalled an update would probably be forthcoming. Eventually, sleep intervened, and he joined the rest of his family, snuggled into the nest of duvets. Sirens and shouts continued outside.

In a muggy alley, the girl leant against a damp wall's flaking paint. Human shadows squatted in doorways rolling dice or sat at plastic tables playing cards. She was supposed to wait. She had swallowed the last mouthful of pop an hour ago and she reckoned she had made the bottle last more than that. She was supposed to wait, but the anger was building up inside. Her mother's voice, twisted by synthetic opium and fake ecstasy—the emotion, not the drug—echoed from an upstairs window. Heads turned toward the source of these rising, piercing cries. Yellow grins, filled with broken teeth, turned to cackle at her.

Suddenly, she was running through the streets of Manila. She reeled through a surreal, claustrophobic world jammed with people and clutter. Clutching hands reached towards her. Shapes in doorways, half lost in the black shadows thrown by the morning sun, followed her with sly eyes. Her mad dash slammed her into a crowd; angry heads turned and glared. A crush of bodies packed around, forcing her to stumble along with them. She felt hysteria rising. The crowd, like an insane confusion of circumstances beyond her control, seemed to jostle her towards some impending tragedy.

She needed safety; a place to hide and be alone. Finally, breaking free of the scrum, her feet took her toward the water. The chaotic interface between land and sea was fractally delineated by floating pontoons and moored vessels. She looked around for a place to hide and slipped under a bundle of oilskins draped over a pile of fishy wooden boxes. She scrambled deep into the heap and found a box big enough to curl up inside. The plastic walls were dotted with shed scales the size of coins. The smell was so intense that, after a few seconds, she failed to sense it.

She used coils of rope as a pillow, intending just to close her eyes and think for a few minutes, to gather herself before plodding back to the brothel, where her mother might soon be finished. She must have slept, though, because as lucidity returned the atmosphere had become unbearable. The sun had risen, heating the air under the tarpaulin, driving moisture from the nets and ropes. The smell was back and the air was tangibly sticky. Although fully awake, she continued to lie still, despite the mounting discomfort. Her mother would be furious, but where else could she go? Trapped, catatonic, fixed by the harbour's web of noise and smell, her unfocused mind spun circles of increasingly limited options.

Suddenly, the yellow plasticised cloth covering the crates jerked. Spears of sunlight jabbed in. Despite her desperate attempts to cling to its edges, the tarpaulin was hauled aside. Terrified, she kicked out and contacted something gristly. The surprised grunt was her signal to writhe like a caterpillar on its back and dash away.

She was running again; darting between crates, cranes, and other nautical chaos. She never managed to get a look at her pursuer, but she did see drops of his blood when she doubled back to make a break for the fish market, a site of maximum confusion. Somewhere she lost him. The shouts and the slapping of sandaled feet slowly disappeared into the general din. She let herself slack off from her frantic dash and wiped the sweat from her forehead with an arm that smelled of fish.

As adrenaline began to wash out, she felt tears welling up. Great sobs tried to force themselves out of her chest. She began to shake. She'd had nothing to eat or drink since she finished her sugary liquid breakfast, and the physical and emotional stress was too much for her eleven-year-old body to bear.

During the chase, she had been running from some degenerate minion sent by her mother to beat her. On cooler reflection, he was more likely just some unfortunate fisherman startled by the feral creature that had broken his nose and taken off like a scalded cat. Even while she had been running for her life, there was some part of her that wanted to be caught. She hated these frightened little girl thoughts; but sitting at the feet of a statue streaked with pigeon shit, she began to focus on her situation and carefully enumerate her options. It didn't take long. Essentially, she had one—two, if she allowed herself to include suicide.

Stella waited there for another half an hour. She considered catching and eating one of the horribly maimed pigeons that hopped around the statue on warty stumps. Eventually, she reluctantly stood and pushed back into the crowd.

Manila was a warren. She had only a basic idea of how to find the brothel where her mother was temping, while the regular girl attended a wedding. It took her hours to find the right street. She finally recognised the face of a man, missing a nose, who apparently hadn't moved from the doorstep where he was begging since Stella went AWOL.

The first furious slap to her face nearly knocked her unconscious, but the half-hearted angry beating that followed quickly turned into a distraught, sobbing cuddle. Knowing that being accosted by this drunken and dishevelled woman was the closest she would get to a mother's love, she hated herself for the numb warmth that filled her chest.

Hours later, after another nightmare of waiting for her mother's last shift to end, they were finally ready to head back to the tuna farm. Stella filled two empty pop bottles with water and packed them into her pink nylon backpack. The brothel owner, an old man with stringy hair and tobacco stained teeth, had given her a sugar bun for the journey. She wrapped it in a crisp packet and tucked it beside the bottles. Her mother took a small box of mangos and three bottles of something Stella was sure wasn't water. They set off on foot back to the harbour. They had arranged to meet one of the service boats that ferried specialists and non-specific cargo between the Farm and any ports within proximity of its course.

Even at night, the plastic pontoons and old masonry docks of the port region seethed with life. Lights, dangling on bare wires, glared and reflected off oily puddles. Automated loaders, bristling with laser range finders and whirling radars, shared the stained old stones with boys pushing carts and stooped, bare-chested drudges.

Stella and her mother were ignored as they pushed through the throng towards a set of concrete steps that led down into the black viscous water. The men had finished loading the cargo an hour ago and were sitting and smoking. They jumped up and started cursing when the two appeared at the top of the steps. Her mother screeched back. She shoved Stella down the stairs before her and onto the already overloaded ten-metre vessel.

They cleared congested waters and headed out to the open sea towards the Farm. Unrelenting waves hammered against the bottom of the aluminium launch, their force shaking the crates, sacks, and bundles lashed together in a heap. Stella's mother lay on the wooden deck, oblivious and insensible under the harsh lights, her skin filmed with toxic sweat.

Guillermo the deck hand, who had been bribed to let them travel with the only thing her mother had to trade, was sitting on a crate doing something to some rope.

"You okay, Stella?" he asked.

Numb with exhaustion, Stella was lost within the receding lights of Manila.

"Stella? You okay girl?"

"Ignore the little cow. She's pissed with me again," her mother's disembodied voice mumbled.

"Fuck you, you filthy old whore!" Stella screamed as the world flickered into focus. She lurched up and flew to the prone woman and began furiously kicking her in the head and tits, screaming all the while. She wanted to kill her, but she was small, and her kicks had little stopping power.

The older woman staggered to her feet, grabbed the small girl like a puppet by the neck and dashed her against the side of the cabin. She would have been beaten blue if Guillermo hadn't intervened, cursing viciously as he flung Stella's mother back onto the heap of rope.

In the far distance, out-of-focus stars and blobs bobbed—a

confusion of blinking masts and towers swaying in the darkness.

Spring followed winter. The riots died down. There was clearly nothing to be gained, and with the sun came a measure of optimism.

"*Mommy* come and look! I can't believe it!" Siegfried was positively vibrating with excitement as he tugged at his mother's sleeve. He pointed at the little piece of earth, where the first of his strawberries had turned from white to red. "We should make milkshake!"

When he heard his son's delightful idea, Anosh looked up from the sweetcorn he was planting and winked at Ayşe. "Good idea, let's get some cows up here too!"

Besides the rows of raised vegetable beds, the roof had acquired a four-ton water tank and a rickety looking windmill. Anosh and Ayşe had spent two hard days scavenging for the wood to build the boxes for the soil beds. They had overturned derelict construction sites in the neighbourhood, salvaging the unused boxy formwork. The kids loved their little garden and were even more excited about the chicken coop Anosh had promised, although it was nothing more than a tangle of wire netting and plywood.

Downstairs, renovations were coming along too. The echoing floor of the old warehouse and ex-printers was still available for mini-tennis, but the southern wall was portioned off into two bedrooms and a lounge/kitchen.

When Anosh finally built his fourth-generation windmill, the "biggest and best yet", he assured Ayşe, they would soon be an exporter of energy. The plan was to barter for naan, bhajis and, optimistically, medicine from the families downstairs.

As the weather improved, vegetables showed up on the shelves again. The appalling rioting had become an embarrassing memory, a hazily remembered event within a rowdy night's drinking; something to be suppressed and forgotten in the light of a new day.

Gradually, people's lives found a new stability. Supermarkets had been nationalised by the new Way Forward government, which now confidently exercised the emergency powers it had awarded itself. The military had viciously put down riots, especially in the north. Scores of the dead had been left on the streets. There had been an outcry; but, in the depths of winter, weakened by the cold and lack of food, the people had allowed themselves to be bribed by emergency rations and persuaded by propaganda that branded protestors as vandals and traitors.

They stayed on the roof, working in their small garden, until a light drizzle forced them back downstairs. While Ayşe made a potato salad, Anosh finished installing some new software on their old router. After a few infuriating false starts and re-installs, he finally saw the sequence of blinking lights that signified a successful boot.

"Hey! We're online!" he called to the others.

"Cool! Can we watch cartoons?" Segi asked immediately.

"No! Let's watch MCBummer!" Zaki insisted.

"Sorry boys, it's just a local network."

Ayşe wandered over. "Zaki, don't try to tell your brother what he should watch."

"I updated the firmware on the router with the new Open-Mesh thumb-drive I got from the market," Anosh said.

"Well, I don't really have any idea what you are talking about, but you look happy, so I'm sure it's good."

He grinned. "We're a telecoms company! The neighbours can link into our Mesh Node. We're sharing telephone and our ePedia, and I'm even thinking about sharing our old movies."

Anosh gave his wife a kiss on the cheek and messed with the boys' hair. At times like these he enjoyed the self-sufficiency that survival, in the face of a gradual slip into anarchy, required. The triumphs made his life meaningful in some small way. Growing vegetables or collecting a few litres of rainwater gave him a satisfaction that the corporate grind had failed to deliver.

There were hardships, too. In the winter, Siegfried had scared them with a bad bout of flu that wouldn't improve. The nights listening to his chest whistling, while he laboured to get enough air, had driven them half-crazy with guilt. They had tried to keep their home warm, but there just wasn't the power or fuel. Eventually, they had obtained some antibiotics through their friends downstairs, and Siegfried had pulled through.

Other families were not so lucky. As the months passed, Prussia slowly adjusted to the millennium's austerity status quo: high unemployment, high energy costs, no more spending outside your means. There were other non-financial costs to their loss in global status. Infant mortality was rising for the first time in three hundred years, as overcrowding at health facilities and shortages of essential medicines brought back diseases like TB and polio.

While the OpenMesh server rebooted again, he set the bandwidth limits and took the external interface online. Now, for the first time in nine months, a sort of internet was available again to the community. Next, he would rig up a directional aerial and scan for other enthusiasts' MeshNodes to spread the love. The breathless hype claimed that, one day, the Mesh would be the people's internet.

They were living through the economic equivalent of the K-T extinction; companies were going bust at an unprecedented rate. As ISPs and backhaul providers had shut down, chunks of the old internet had gone dark. What was left became congested, and bandwidth, when available, came at an increasingly high price. The paranoid accused the new Way Forward government of deliberately sabotaging communications to prevent the people from organising challenges to its increasingly paternal regime. Anosh tended to believe the rumours; certainly, the government had shown no enthusiasm for restoring the flow of information. The internet had become an expensive and restrictive luxury.

But, like nimble mammals emerging from under the oppressive corpses of decaying behemoths, thousands of local networks were springing up. Unlike the internet—exclusive, expensive, unreliable, censored, and hobbled by the mandatory spyware that ran amok across its pay per byte network of routers—this Mesh would belong to the people.

The OpenMesh software linked all the little networks. It spread organically, peer to peer, via the USB drives sold or given away at demonstrations. Even before the recent recessions, the hacktivist community had started

working on an alternative to what they felt had become a symbol of oppressive government control. Internet access required a Citizen's ID. With all actions logged, archived, and traceable, people began to self-censor. Gone were the late night searches for [*Insert Your Fetish of Choice Here*]. The Mesh was the alternative, an organism spreading its mycelia through society's disenfranchised rotting stump.

Routers were piped into old modems. They broadcast bits via CB radio or carried the reborn networks from one town to the next on fibres buried beside roads or threaded through sewers.

OpenMesh was a Fully Autonomous Corporation. A distributed digital corporation without management. Running its programs on your hardware made you an employee. Decentralised algorithms paid you in the Mesh's own Crypto Currency—MeshCoin—which customers used as payment to send data through its network.

Anosh watched the lights flicker as foreign interfaces shook hands with this little box of magic, pinging, probing, tracing. The air was full of packets caught and spat out again. He logged into the router admin console and was unrealistically disappointed to see nobody had signed up for his film service yet. The computers, tablets, and phones out there had almost instantly latched onto the new network, but it would take a while for the humans, operating on very different timescales, to learn of his offers.

This felt like the future. One day, the Mesh would girdle the world. Every mobile phone, laptop, and router would act as a node. Already, if Anosh could find his way onto one of its twigs, their packets could travel hundreds of kilometres, without going near the crumbling relic that was the internet.

The rest of the family had drifted off to more exciting activities, except for Segi. Siegfried, as his mother still insisted on calling him, was happy just to sit on his father's lap and look at the lights flashing. Anosh, his knees protesting, stood and let the boy slide off. He gave him a playful push and they walked to the window. From there, they could look out over the old docks towards the lights of the city across the Rheine.

The view was practically the same as from Anosh's old office. He remembered it well from all his uncompensated nights of overtime. The cityscape was a ghost of its former self, as if someone had turned up the transparency of the city to let the black night behind seep through. Years previously, the price of power had been so insignificant that offices left lights burning all night and streetlights flooded the ground and sky with a dirty orange glow. At least the sky was black again and they could enjoy the stars.

Anosh pointed up at a bright, soft orange point. "Look, Segi. That's Mars… Do you remember the name of our sister planet?"

"Yes Dad. It's Venus!"

"Okay, and what about that one?"

"That's a planet?"

Anosh nodded.

"Jupiter?"

"Not bad. No, it's Saturn, but I only know because I just checked."

Siegfried pointed at a bright star drifting smoothly across the night. Anosh followed the point until it faded. The deserted shell of the GSS was still circling the Earth in endless free-fall. Its fuel was running low and soon it would dip too deep into the atmosphere's thin upper reaches and be dragged down to disintegrate and burn up. These days, in the midst of the Global Economic Depression, rocket launches couldn't be justified. There were simply too many other more pressing priorities. At least it would provide the ambivalent people below with a firework display.

A few days later, their new Mesh connection proved its worth when it brought them a rumour of fresh fruit. By the time Ayşe arrived, the queue already stretched at least 200 metres up the street and around a corner. It was a fairly good-natured line-up. The Mesh rumour claimed the government delivery truck had offloaded at least thirty boxes; and, at an allocation of two oranges per body, there should be enough for everybody in the line today. She had dragged both the boys with her to make sure they got their share.

The boys were off playing somewhere in the queue with some other children. Ayşe hated that. Hated the possibility she would lose her place if she had to go chasing after them. She also knew she couldn't keep them standing next to her for what might be three hours, without them driving her crazy.

She was standing behind a chubby lady with a scarf wrapped over her head and big rubber boots on her feet. The woman scowled at Ayşe whenever the kids made a noise. Possibly, she was jealous of the four extra oranges the boys represented. In front of her, a couple of neighbours from across the road waited: a young man and his girlfriend. Ayşe chatted to the woman occasionally, while the young man passed the time playing something mindless on his Companion.

"Did you get any of the bananas last week?" the man asked.

"Yes, lovely weren't they?"

"I suppose they were. Not enough fruit though, is there?"

"I try to plant a lot of spinach and kale," said Ayşe, "so I have something to feed those two. But a little more fruit would be nice."

"Do you have a garden?" the young man asked. People nearby turned at something in his voice.

Ayşe knew that, if Anosh were here, he would be kicking her under the proverbial table.

"No, just window boxes," she lied and the guy lost interest.

Eventually, they got to the front of the line and she accepted her six big oranges, a kilogram of flour, a bag of potatoes, and two pathetic-looking leaks. There was no butter or milk again.

"Can we go home now?" Zaki asked.

"Yes darling. Do you want to push the shopping cart?"

"No. Siegfried can do it."

"Zaki! At least take it in turns, okay?"

"Okay, Mama."

They set off back up the line, which did not seem any shorter. People were getting tense; they were no longer sure the supply would last. A group of youths were hanging around at the crossing that Ayşe would usually have taken. Instead, she steered them another way. She waited for Zaki to get control of the cart, which was basically a wooden box with the wheels from Siegfried's old push chair screwed to its sides. Eventually, they reached the docks, then their neighbourhood, and finally their building—or, as Ayşe was surprised to find herself thinking these days: home.

The Farm was a ring of buoys and pontoons three hundred metres in diameter. Hanging from this floating hoop, a vast net basket dangled a hundred metres towards the dark depths below. This basket of rings, hoops and rope created a pen for a fortune in tuna. The extinction of tuna in the wild had created a massive market for premium farmed Sashimi. The current harvest consisted of Yellow Eye: a fast-growing, high-fat, GM species, developed especially for the Munisai Sushi chain.

Over the years, the Farm's surface structure had become encrusted with its own population of terrestrial parasites and symbionts. The three-metre-wide service walkway that followed the circumference was lined with shanty hovels, shops and gardens. A small flotilla of miscellaneous vessels hung around its waters or moored to its pontoons. One section of the huge ring supported a cluster of official buildings that towered over the rest of the floating ghetto on thick legs, five metres tall. The height provided a refuge from the huge waves that periodically lashed the rest of the structure.

Stella and her mother lived at the Pussy Cat Club, a permanent aggregate of plastic and wood, built between the legs of the canteen building. It enjoyed a reputation that extended beyond the Farm, attracting business from passing merchant and pirate vessels, even enticing the odd adventurous excursion from dry land. Like most of the ad hoc construction on the Farm, empty two-ton feed bins figured prominently in its structure. Every couple of years, a huge storm would scrub the encrustation from the Farm, leaving it as close to its factory spec as it ever got. At these times, the blue feed drums were the hardy spoors from which the colony could re-grow. One short person could sleep comfortably inside a drum. Two people could share one for a brief intimate encounter. During a storm, three or four had been known to cram in, hoping, as the less resilient buildings were washed into the sea, the ties holding the drum to the superstructure would hold.

Stella's own pod was around the back of the Pussy Cat, above the smelly shortcut between the pigs and chickens. The guano that slathered its weathered plastic marked it as one of the Farm's oldest epiphytic structures.

The Farm was like a medieval village floating in a great, lazy circle around the Pacific. The workers and squatters were its peons. The management were its lords. Reefers would come and moor alongside the fish factory, where the Yellow Eyes were harvested and loaded. Catching them was literally shooting fish in a barrel. Tuna were herded to the surface by the Farm's RVs and dispatched with headshots from a small coil gun mounted to the deck. The bringer of death sent high-velocity, super cavitation rounds fizzing through the water to punch through thick scales and bones. Slowly sinking carcasses were gathered up by dexterous little RVs and hauled into the flash freezers.

The kids on the Farm were their own tribe. Parents were mostly too poor, ignorant, or drug dependent to look after their offspring properly; but, despite the neglect, the environment was mostly benign. The corporation that ran it, a Nipponese/Prussian conglomerate, was as socially aware as the fiercely competitive environment of twenty-first century capitalism would allow. The mostly Nipponese management team was fair, providing food and basic medicines; and, although the diet had a strongly fishy theme, it was high in Omega-3, and it kept the kids nourished and healthy.

The Farm received and processed organic waste delivered by vast tankers. The sewage was bought fit for the human food chain, mercury-free and sterilised by ionising radiation to kill bacteria and viruses. The precious stinking filth was released in trickles into the smallest pen at the centre, where it was consumed by algae and phyto-plankton. Portals in the fine mesh allowed this biological broth to wash slowly into the second pen, where small fish and fry ate it. These could swim out and away from safety into the third and fourth pens, where they fed the VIP residents: two-ton tubes of protein that were top of the pelagic food chain, and second only to whale meat as the most prestigious and expensive food on the planet. Fishing was restricted within the Farm, but the management tolerated the kids catching a few little fish and squid as they swam in the tuna pens.

The school held its lessons in the workers' canteen building between meal times. Today, it smelled of cabbage. An older, ossified mind might shatter under the stress and abuse that surrounded Stella Sagong. But she still retained enough of a child's point of view that the bad memories faded fast. The class was a mix of girls and boys between nine and thirteen, and Stella was one of the oldest.

Ms Wassen, their history teacher, was talking about Charles the First, some English king who had been beheaded. Marcel and the other boys were riveted, but Stella found it all a bit dull. The teacher kept repeating herself, trying to get some point across, which Stella found especially tedious. The boys just wanted to hear about the blood and whether he could still see when his head was off.

The white plastic table where she sat hadn't been properly wiped, and there were salt grains scattered across its surface. Stella herded them into little piles and stared out of the window.

"…you see, the people insisted their king must be accountable to the law…"

A small ball of paper and spit flew past her ear and stuck onto the window. Ms Wassen pretended not to notice. Stella turned around and glared at the chuckling boys, who were both chewing as they prepared the next batch of projectiles.

"…and trace a theme through the next four hundred years…"

Stella lost interest with the salt and picked at the scabs on her knee instead.

Jihng put her hand up. "Miss Wassen, why we don't have real kings anymore?"

"Who are *we*, Jihng?"

"Us Miss, anybody I suppose?"

"Well, the English have a king, but he doesn't have much power, it's true. But some, like the Arabs, still have real kings."

"And the King of the Sea?" Marcel asked.

"He means Mr Munisai, Miss. That's what we call him, Ma'am. The King of the Sea," Jihng explained.

"Well no, Marcel, he's not a king, just a very rich old man. It's just a name people sometimes call him."

"But Miss…" Marcel stuck his hand in the air and jiggled on his seat impatiently, waiting to be acknowledged. "He has a castle by the sea! And he owns all this…" In a wide gesture, Marcel seemed to take in the room, the people and, perhaps, the entire surrounding ocean.

"A castle does not a king make!" the elderly lady replied with a wry smile.

"What? Why can't we have a king, Miss? Like in the Mermaid Princess, Miss? A king would look after us."

"That's enough now, Lixue! From what I've heard, Mr Munisai doesn't sound like a very nice old man, and he's certainly not a king, and I think we are lucky for that at least! Your father works for him; the least he could do is send you a new pair of shorts without holes or a bit more fruit! Now, let's get back to poor King Charles."

An hour later, they had a test. Stella came first. Jihng probably wouldn't talk to her for a week now. After the lesson, the fifteen kids of the middle school dashed out of the classroom. In their haste they pushed past the dinner ladies, who were arriving to prepare the crew's evening meal.

"Want to catch some shrimps?" Marcel asked from amongst the mini-throng.

Stella had nothing better to do. "Why not? I know where we can go. There were loads of them last week when I looked."

"No, follow me."

Marcel was usually happy to go along with Stella's suggestions; but she had learnt, long ago, if he insisted, he usually had a good reason. She agreed, and they headed to one of the pontoons that stuck out of the rim like multiple handles from a giant mutant ping-pong bat.

They were close to the equator, and it was about thirty-five degrees centigrade with a brisk, moist wind. Shirtless and without a trace of shyness, Marcel stepped out of his shorts and stood in his underpants, grinning.

"Coming?"

Last year, Stella would probably have stripped to her underwear and joined him. Now, even though she thought of Marcel as practically a brother, it didn't feel right.

"I'll just climb down the ladder and hold the bucket."

Marcel shrugged and immediately dived from the pontoon. He gracefully traversed two metres of air and passed through the water's interface with barely a splash. He swam back. Stella passed him the net. The trick was to dive below the bottom of the pontoon, where great clumps of seaweed hung down into the water, and run the net through the weed. The big shrimps, startled by the net, flipped away from the wooden bar at the front and, hopefully, ended up in the net. If you were quick and lucky, you could trap them before they escaped.

Marcel passed up the spiky crustaceans, one at a time, and Stella plopped them into the bucket, keeping the lid down to stop them from jumping out. She had been right to trust his choice of fishing spot. After an hour, Marcel had caught about twenty of the big prawns and far more of the smaller shrimps. They grilled a few big ones on a piece of sheet metal the sun had heated until it was too hot to touch. Then, they ate the delicious sweet flesh, while sitting with their feet in the water, watching the churning shoals of little fish that materialised to glean the discarded scraps of shell.

Contemplative, docile, uncharacteristically calm for once, he let the Companion flop from his fingers onto his lap, and he sat staring at the horizon. Punt was Disney Land quaint. All marble, sandstone, and golden Byzantine domes, the hotel was set high on the slopes of Ras Syan, chiselled into the red stone, filled with tinkling fountains and dotted with palm trees. It was reachable up a thousand convincingly worn stairs that threaded through the terraced chaos of the 'Old Town'. Alternatively, escalators pierced the rock, linking the surface town to the many air-conditioned artificial caverns that riddled the hill.

The city had been built in an epic surge of construction by the first of the new Caliphs, who had needed to cement the extremity of his empire onto the horn of Africa. Out to sea, the colossal concrete stakes, between which the spans of the Bab-el-Mandeb bridge would one day hang, marched off towards Arabia. When completed, Punt would be the gateway house, linking the Caliphate's northern and southern estates. It was already the Caliph's administrative capital for the entire continent.

He looked down on the chaotic roofs below. The maddening disorder of the 'Old Town' had been built first in zeros and ones by simulating a thousand years of commerce and organic development. Only when forty generations of virtual peasants had lived their imitation lives was it caused to manifest into the tangible world of atoms. Massive, crawling insectile machines had extruded a mixture of sand and lime from which the walls and roofs of the city had slowly grown, layer by layer. The impression was of an ancient Kasbah that had risen out of the sea and draped itself across the little mountain.

Passively, he let his eyes flick across the cobalt wedge of water in jumps and starts, pausing on the ochre blurs of islands and flicking between the small shapes of fishing boats and yachts that speckled the bay. He gazed over the gulf of Bab-el-Mandeb and toward the faint bar, lost in haze, that might be the far shore of the Gate of Tears.

A cruise ship was moored offshore and, even at this distance, he could see the multitude of tiny garish skiffs leaving its sleek silhouette, to carry the curious back in time. He didn't need his eyes to picture the hawkers, 'looky-looky' men, beggars, cripples, whores, porters, would-be slaves, refugees and every other example of desperate human ingenuity, converging on the rich feast.

Effluence drawn to Affluence, he thought to himself.

This was where mankind had left its first cradle. One hundred thousand years ago, newly minted Homo sapiens crossed the same short distance that his eyes had just traversed in a couple of hops.

His gaze, now guided by a message from even further back in time, jumped again and came to rest on the tits of the woman lying on the next balcony. Nice. Small and evenly tanned, tiny glistening beads of sweat formed between them where their swell stilled the wind and slowed evaporation. His eyes followed a chain of features: the soft hollow of her solar plexus; a succession of tiny silky fair hairs contrasting with her tanned stomach; the perfection of her navel; then, his eyes seemingly unable to pace themselves any longer, straight to the camel's toe.

He stood suddenly. The Companion clattered to the tiles. Ben was now anything but relaxed; 'pre-coital' might more accurately describe his condition. He couldn't think of an opening gambit with the tits on the neighbouring balcony that would allow the desired traversal of social space, so he set off for the bar, where the social topology was more conducive and the transitions better mapped.

Ben had been in Djibouti for six days and was gradually learning its ways. It was early afternoon, and the people in the hotel bar in the early afternoon tended to fall into a small set of well-defined classes. This would further restrict the dimensionality of the 'pick-up phase space', allowing him to skip the tedious iterative stage of snubs and slaps and directly select an optimal starting location.

***

"Dry Martini for the lady," the waiter said, placing a small black doily on the bar and centring the glass on top.

The mythical breasts from the balcony were still fresh in his mind, so it was a minor disappointment these were so large and soft—and orange. Yet, they were undeniably breasts. The body, from the tips of its pink toenails to the top of its tightly-permed hair, with all the expanses of orange flesh between, was undeniably female; and that was, after all, the point.

"Nice tan," he said.

"Oh, thanks," she replied with apparent sincerity, entirely missing any implied sarcasm. His subconscious incorporated this latest titbit and pruned off several more scenarios.

She lifted the conical glass to her purple lips and smiled with her eyes at him over its rim, while hooking the olive with her exceedingly dexterous tongue.

The number of potential end-states for this interaction was rapidly approaching one. So, with some annoyance, Ben answered his phone, which had just started chirping and vibrating around in his pocket.

"Sure, no problem. I can be on my way in forty minutes... Okay, sure, I will be there in forty minutes... yes I am at work... Okay, okay, fuck, I'm leaving now!"

"Oww, have you got to go away?" she said in her best 'daddy's little girl' voice.

"No, it's nothing. You want to go for a little drive, see the city a bit?"

"Sure." Her glass was emptied and her purse snatched up in one practised movement, then she was on her feet and ready to go.

Already on his way to the door, he reached back, closed his hand around her plump fingers, and piloted them out of the gloom into the blinding light. They entered an old sandstone gatehouse set into the side of the mountain, got onto the escalator, dropped three floors, then took the lift down to the auto park.

The auto was cruising along the dual carriageway, driving itself so the humans could concentrate on more important matters. He hadn't bothered to dial the windows to opaque. She hadn't noticed or didn't care. His seat was fully reclined and she was bumping and grinding away, holding onto the sides of the open sunroof for stability and whooping from time to time with enthusiasm. After ten minutes, they left the main autobahn and entered the winding streets of old Djibouti City. The antiquity passing by their windows was genuine now. The cobbled roads were uneven and scattered with potholes. She grinned down at him, reached back to the console and dialled the suspension to sport mode. The hardened suspension transmitted the vibrations very effectively from road to flesh.

"Not the first time you've been in a Benz then?" he said.

She grinned again and settled into a determined rhythm for the final straight. The streets were much narrower here; more importantly, this was where he was meeting his contact. They drove the last few blocks with windows blackened.

***

A man watched the progress of the black Benz as it edged forward, gently nudging through the throng of pedestrians swarming the streets, a mix of tourists and locals. The locals, he knew, were all some vague blend of historical re-enactor and petty criminal. The road was quaintly uneven, but this did not seem sufficient to explain the severe amount of rocking and swaying going on with the car. An astute observer could postulate the rocking might have something to do with the head bobbing up occasionally through the sunroof. Two minutes after it pulled to a halt, the door opened and the owner of the head stepped out, followed by Ben Baphmet. Both spent a few seconds tucking loose clothing back in and sealing fasteners.

On the pavement below, the process of polite disengagement began.

"Shall I get the car to drop you somewhere?"

"Look at you... the last of the gentlemen!" She seemed genuinely impressed. "The Red Cat in the Hilton is always fun at this time of day."

"You got that car?" Ben said.

"Yes, Mr Baphmet," the Benz replied.

"Okay, I've got to dash, go have fun!"

"Sure Honey, thanks for the *ride*." She winked.

She had already climbed into the back and was exploring the contents of the refreshment console. She blew him a little kiss and winked as the car pulled away. A pale, troubled man in a cheap polyester suit had joined them and watched the car slip back into the crowd.

"Jesus Ben, what the fuck was that?" he said.

"A little afternoon delight." Ben winked back and took the moistened towelette that his colleague was offering. He worked on some of the purple lipstick and orange chemotan that was plastered over his face and collar.

"Your father was fuming on the phone just now!" said the

man. "He said he needs you on the six o'clock flight to Johannesburg and that you need to put Al-Afaf straight first."

"He'll live. What's all this about?" Ben asked. "I was supposed to meet him tomorrow."

"Your father had Wallace move it up. Apparently the deal is looking very fragile."

"Well, that's why I'm here, right?" Ben quipped. He was feeling pretty pumped right now.

"Sure *that's* why you're here," Shaun said, adding quietly, "not because your daddy owns the company."

"Fuck you, Shaun! You wanna get re-assigned to fucking Manchester or something? Open the fucking door and tell Mr Al-Afaf I'm on my way."

Even as a joke, it was not a threat to be taken lightly, and Shaun rushed to hold open the door to the Caliphate government building.

Adil Afif Al-Afaf stepped back from his window and sighed melodramatically. The heavy curtains fell back over the windows; the slab of white light, projecting onto the blue and crimson carpet, shrank, and the room returned to its normal gloomy state.

Life is not fair. The rich get richer; the poor get poorer. Change is always around the corner, and the chance of a better future just out of reach. The paradox of progress is that innovation always looks like a threat to those doing well today, while it is like a chance at a better tomorrow for those with nothing. The truly powerful recognise that each invention is another niche to be exploited. Regardless of the intended purpose of each new piece of technology or regulation, in practice it will add complexity to the environment: up the stakes and shift advantage relentlessly towards the smart end of the spectrum.

Even in something as dry and structured as mathematics there will inevitably be contradictions and inconsistencies. The infinitely sloppier system of international laws is a damp dishcloth of opportunity, ripe for infestation by keen young legal minds in the service of their corporate masters.

Bio-diversity was once a barren terrain populated mainly by fans of corduroy trousers and camper vans. Now it was big business, a massive steaming heap of treaties and laws. One particularly fecund niche comprised the Recognising Economic Value of Beneficial Species act—REVOBS. It was created to stop the plundering of the commons by compensating species for services rendered. Pollination by honeybees had been the poster child. Why shouldn't their economically vital work be compensated? Rights had been auctioned off in a massive species land grab. Nobody had bid against Al-Afaf.

The office was cool and dark. Sunlight slid into the room through slits in the heavy maroon velvet curtains. Where it fell, it illuminated the ancient creamy marble tiles, penetrating beneath the translucent stones' surface and lighting them from within.

"Mr Baphmet, do I have to remind you that we contribute thirty trillion ECUs a year to your client's books?"

The air was too warm and far too moist. Three walls were covered in wallpaper that continued the maroon velvet theme. Disturbingly oversized antique etchings of Al-Afaf's clients hung in gilt frames from the walls.

"Well, thirty trillion isn't what it once was, right? Frankly, I think you're over-reacting. We are not re-negotiating existing contracts; the European and American development projects will continue to utilise your clients' services. We're still happy with the agreed share of the ecosystem subsidies your clients are entitled to from the UN."

Ben didn't like Afaf's contrived 'lawyer to family Dracula' style, especially the childish decor of his office. 'Slimy little shit,' he thought as his eyes jumped from one grotesque image to the next.

"The ruling is this weekend," Ben continued. "Çin will decide on the core ecosystem composition of the site. *If* your clients are given aboriginal first tier status, then we will happily extend our agreement."

Al-Afaf was starting to whine: "We provide a vital role in any healthy wetland habitat. I can hardly believe you would risk the stability of your site's environment by eco-engineering your way around our niche! The UN granted us wetland, tundra, and river delta first tier primary consumer status!"

"After heavy lobbying from your firm."

"We submitted an impartial scientific analysis to the UN, just like Apis Inc. and Lepidoptera Consolidated, and several other trusts. Nobody is talking about squeezing them out."

"Çin never ratified those treaties; they voluntarily adhere to some aspects. Not big tree huggers, the Slopes. Also, some big party names are considering purchases on our site. One rather influential party head is pushing to classify your little guys as parasites to get them cut from the first tier list."

The fourth wall behind the desk was a sheet of glass bisecting the room, isolating its last metre. The lower thirty centimetres of this space was filled with murky water, which was lit from below so the wriggling larval stages of Al-Afaf's clients cast sick, oversized shadows onto a back wall, which had been left a clean creamy white to enhance the effect. The air above was thick with adults.

"As the site developer, any recommendations you make will almost certainly be accepted by the sovereign authorities," Afaf whined, wringing his hands. "Surely our longstanding and profitable relationship counts for something, even in these decadent times?"

"If Çin classifies the mosquito as a human parasite, we will be free to find an alternative provider for the fish and amphibian food niche." Ben looked him in the eye. "Cutting all the marketing crap, nobody likes a blood-sucker, Mr Al-Afaf. Your average Çin oligarch is reluctant to pay in money and blood just to feed their fish. They're looking into alternatives."

Al-Afaf leant forward on his elbows. "And I suppose you have an alternative in mind?"

"Well, there are apparently some South American water snails that also feed on planktonic algae and lay copious numbers of seemingly delicious eggs."

"You know we don't represent molluscs," the little man said with some distaste. "So, the fact that you are even here tells me you have another option for me, Mr Baphmet?"

"My client has acquired the rights of a new GM variant."

"Based on?"

Ben was young, impulsive and irresponsible, but was good at his job. He knew Al-Afaf needed this contract and now was time for the carrot.

"The modification is compatible with a wide range of species, including the genomes you represent."

"I see…" Smelling a compromise, Al-Afaf leant back further in his chair. He stretched his thin arms forward to rest his fingers on the edge of the desk and peered intently at Ben over his half-moon glasses. "What is the modification?"

Ben's eyes glazed over slightly as he concentrated on the voice that his Spex whispered in his ear:

"An auto immune cascade reaction triggered in response to uniquely primate blood proteins," Ben explained, repeating the contextual prompts. "The modifications are all placed in critical reproductive areas, on multiple chromosomes, making it highly unlikely that random mutations will remove the traits. Also, our strain hyper-expresses sexual selection markers, making it a preferable mate for the wild type. Hybrids are guaranteed to inherit the modification. The *cut* will shift the fitness topology to favour individuals who avoid food that contains the selected proteins."

"I am a lawyer, Mr Baphmet, not a geneticist," said Al-Afaf, "but I think I understand you want to make my mosquitoes allergic to human blood?"

"Yeah, and the hard work has already been done. Now *our* client would like to help you by listing this new strain of *your* clients as a core participant in all his ecosystem specifications for existing and future development sites. With the parasite ruling from Çin, we should have a legal basis for the modification. They would be happy to share revenues generated on a fifty-fifty basis. The vehicle would be Culico Corp; our client already runs a lot of their GM licencing through it."

"Nonsense! your modifications are merely a tweak! You can't ignore two hundred million years of evolution. Eighty-twenty would be more reasonable."

"In controlled trials, after just eight generations, wild populations of mozzies stopped biting people. The boffins are looking into the mechanism, but it seems robust. Think of the adoption rates you will see! Projects across the world will be queuing up to reintroduce your clients. You might even take back sub-Saharan Africa!"

"Sixty-forty and you sign over all patents and other intellectual property to us; otherwise, we will bring an unlicensed modification suit against your client."

Ben smiled and stuck out his hand.

"Deal!" His Spex would have recorded the entire conversation and the shake constituted a legally binding acceptance of the terms of the contract. "I'll get my office to draft up the legal and mail it over."

Ben had just given Al-Afaf a PR coup and probably doubled his firm's annual licensing revenue; but, as Al-Afaf limply gripped the proffered hand and the reality of a world free of biting mosquitoes sunk in, he looked like a kid with a broken toy. He would probably have to re-model his office and abandon his stupid gothic styling.

Humans have their castes. These are the archetypes familiar from myth and fiction. In the male medieval world view, they might be called: fool, warrior, serf, sage, and king. Evolution plays a collectable card game with itself over eons. Each new generation is dealt from the deck to make a hand the size of a typical cro-magnon village. The proportions of the archetypes in the deck represent the composition of the society. A village of mostly serfs, with insufficient warriors, will enjoy a peaceful agrarian existence for a few turns, until inevitable carnage and extermination visits from outside. Some neighbouring village, strong on warrior cards or with advanced technology from wise old sages, will smash its huts, kill the children, and plough the resulting offal back into the pack.

The sage seeks wisdom for its own sake, only as a side effect turning up useful principles and widgets for the king, who cares nothing for any concept of abstract truth. To him, all information is a tool for conquest or repression.

After a long game, having ultimately prevailed through superior weapons and tactics enabled by his educated society, the winning king will have a hand strong on sages and hermits and will find himself with the peacetime problem of herding cats. His ideology does not fit into any universal truth; his policies are self-serving and sub-optimal. After all the battles are won, he can no longer afford to fund the arcane hobbies of his sages or support what goes on within the dungeons beneath the alchemist's towers. This will annoy these inquisitive, idealistic, and politically naive nerds.

A successful king must react to the danger inherent in a mass of educated and dissatisfied, potential troublemakers. He must redirect their perilous energy inwards, away from the relentless need to uncover destabilising truths, towards something absorbing and pacifying. The standard option is a theology fascinating enough that it will draw in successive generations of troublesome intellectuals to work on its vast, pointless mandala.

Not that any of this is conscious in the mind of the king. History is evolution. The bad choices will simply disappear, leaving only those who succeed. Winning strategies can be adopted by observing what works, with no understanding of why.

Christianity, which replaced classical philosophy as the primary sink for intellectual activity when the Romans became the Roman Catholics, was a fantastically mysterious bundle of lore containing enough metaphor, logic, and mystery to support a thousand years of intellectual masturbation. It was a beautiful time of limited destabilisation for the ruling classes. Eventually, the marrow was sucked from the bone and brilliant minds found its patterns familiar and faded. The mysteries became inconsistencies. Luther showed that faith didn't require the intermediary of the Catholic Church. The new Renaissance man went further. He was enticed by the possibility of bypassing revealed knowledge altogether and stealing fire directly from the gods—one patiently validated insight at a time.

Physics and chemistry first, then messy biology following. Obsessive pedants sorted the rules and multitudes of life into neat piles. Mind, the most nonlinear, recursive, and baffling of domains, remained the zealously guarded purview of priests and mystics until the twentieth century.

Biologists, used to sorting, collecting, and pinning their specimens to boards, were the first to attack the rainbow of minds from the edges, starting with the broken and defective. Scientists in the new field of psychology zapped, hacked, and drugged their way through tens of thousands of patients. They assembled crude maps of the brain along the way, and didn't stop until there was a name for everything they considered a departure from the median: Asperger's, ADS, Dyslexia, and Homosexuality... A box, and often a profitable prescription drug, was created for each.

Most divergent from human understanding were the minds of the animals. A blinkered, solipsistic, insanity prevailed for most of the twentieth century, which insisted if it cannot be objectively measured it is not science and, therefore, impossible to describe with meaningful statements. Animals were not conscious; how could they be if it was not measurable?

"I eat this ice-cream because I like its flavour, but this monkey screams when I rub acid into its eyes because the scream is an evolutionary adaptation that confers a selective advantage on the species by warning other members of a present danger."

This arrogance is a variant of: "I know I am conscious, but what about you?"

The dying of old ossified brains in the early twenty-first century—

"Truth does not triumph by convincing its opponents, but rather, because its opponents eventually die."

—brought a softening of this solipsistic dogma. Primates, with their anthropomorphic hands and faces, were recognised by the more progressive judicial systems as people. Dolphins and parrots, with their firm grasp of language, were accepted as being self-aware. When tested for mathematical or linguistic ability, most animals proved surprisingly smart. However, apart from the parrots, they couldn't communicate in our language, and we were usually worse in theirs.

Language allows ideas to exist outside of brains. During the hundreds of thousands of years before early Homo acquired language, our bones evolved faster than our technology. For over half a million years, hand axes remained essentially unchanged, while teeth and bones metamorphosed from ape to man. Without language, even the most brilliant agents are doomed to repeat the discoveries and errors of their ancestors.

Ape + Language = Human Being.

***

Hot air carrying organic smells blew steadily up from the station and tussled the tufts of hair that poked out from under Keith's baseball cap. The warmth was nice, the smells less so. He jogged down a few cracked yellow tiled steps and pushed through a small scruffy crowd, who were also enjoying the warmth while they milled around in front of the ticket barriers. The desperate huddle shuffled out of the way as Keith approached. Before the barrier beeped and sprang open he was subjected to a brief, almost overpowering, encounter with super-strength beer fumes. The gate shut again after he passed, separating legitimate travellers from thermal tourists.

It was after 10am and the morning rush was over, so the station was deserted. Keith followed the familiar tunnels to the platform, where a few other travellers were sitting or standing. He looked up at the long-dead information board. It was as blank as it had been for the past five years, but he didn't need to get out his Companion or check his watch or resort to any of the other cybernetic oracles at his disposal to understand he had just missed the previous train.

Various forms of economic and political propaganda covered the walls, each plastered upon another, building up thick mâché strata. In places, the weight of paper had pulled itself off the wall, sometimes revealing the scratched old inactive video screens below. The structure and the superficial layers of adverts and announcements charted the social trajectory of London. They captured proud Victorian wrought iron and hand-enamelled tiles; massively chunky seventies surveillance cameras, still hanging uselessly from ceiling-mounted poles; early twenty-first century flat screens that had once beckoned from every surface. Now, two massive poster-sized screens looked down on the platform and fed news and previews from upcoming shows to those who couldn't afford Spex.

Keith watched the huge screens distractedly, where a well-groomed young man in a wetsuit interviewed a dolphin, using some new language translation software. Keith couldn't get the gist of the interview. The interviewer seemed to ask why the dolphin had written a book attacking humanity. A man on the platform was standing in the way, blocking the subtitles, so Keith couldn't catch the answer. There hadn't been a train for at least ten minutes and the platform was slowly filling up.

A crude hanged man and the slogan 'Fletcher should die' was spray-painted onto an old yellowing underground map. For a few seconds, Keith was surprised at the audacity, as any street artist working down here was almost guaranteed to be caught by London Transport's vigilance and ubiquitous smelling, watching, and listening. Then, he figured it was just more cunning propaganda.

Although Keith didn't follow the soaps, he knew Fletcher was a gang lord in one of the alternative reality shows. He recalled this one was set in a fictional dystopian London, where honest, hardworking people struggled against crime syndicates with ties to corrupt officials. Keith chuckled at the irony. Surprised for having been caught out, he wondered what else amongst the degenerate squalor was sophisticated stage dressing designed to subconsciously prime him for some long scam. Even as he looked down on the mentally lazy *sheeple*, who followed the trash pumped out by the RBC or syndicated through the networks, he knew it was only with a constant effort of conscious filtering that he kept his own worldview intact.

News shows deliberately mixed stories from fictitious versions of London with the real deal, and most people who watched did not have the mental discipline to separate fact from fiction. They relaxed and allowed the deceptions to wash over them.

Bodies were crammed in around him; it had been forty minutes. A distant screech and wad of approaching air finally announced a train.

While he was being funnelled in through the door, he took in the battered old aluminium carriage, its faded orange tartan seats, and wooden planks showing through the worn linoleum. He wondered at the layers of deceit it represented. Keith thought he understood the world: too many people, too much incompetence, not enough good old blitz spirit. Was this *his* analysis, or were subtle nudges guiding his thinking?

***

"Morning, Mr Wilson, I hope you had a pleasant journey. Would you like a glass of water or a coffee?"

Keith looked up to see a pretty admin in a tight-fitting, but smart, blue business dress. She was reading from a Companion tablet, probably showing his picture and biography and the details of the morning's meetings.

"Hi, sure, a coffee. That would be great."

Keith's eyes lingered as she turned and walked away to source him a cup of coffee, but he quickly lowered them, acutely aware his gaze and entire physiological state was almost certainly being scrutinised as he waited. The coffee hadn't arrived when she returned and told him they were ready for him. Cruel, his body's Pavlovian reaction to the offer of coffee, now unceremoniously retracted, rattled him. He felt as if he was losing composure, just when he needed it most. Keith picked up his man-bag and followed, his gaze intently fixed on the back of the girl's neck. He was relying solely on peripheral vision to inform him of the pleasing way her hips swayed as she walked.

They padded along the richly carpeted corridors, past conference rooms and offices. She stopped at a door, knocked politely; then, turning the handle, she gently pushed the door open for Keith.

"Good luck, see you in a half hour," she said smiling politely, before walking back the way they had come.

The occupant of the office, a smartly dressed young man about Keith's age, dashed around his desk and across the room. He leant out of the door to observe the departure of the admin.

"Ha! Keith! Come in, how are you?"

"Hi Ben, I'm fine. How are you? How's the job?"

"Good to hear. The job's great. I'm great. Just got back from fucking Somalia. Ever been there? Bat-shit crazy I tell you."

Ben put a paternal arm around Keith's shoulders and guided him into the office. It was spacious and simple, with low-key geometric art and subtle lighting. One wall showed a low-resolution scene of apparent rural bliss: a group of boys in whites playing cricket. There were formal neo-classical buildings in the background. Something about the scene was unpleasantly familiar to Keith. Despite the green grass, white-clad children, and fluffy clouds, it evoked a vague sense of dread.

"Drink?" Ben asked.

"Coffee, thanks. I did ask the receptionist…"

"Ha! And did you get any? You think she's allowed to dole out coffee to any old pleb, Keith?" Ben chuckled. "Michelle, coffee for two," he said to the room.

"Hey, look at this. I was just doing some research on a prospective candidate," Ben added cryptically, while gesturing for play to resume.

Keith realised the scene on the wall was a frozen frame from a video. As the video un-paused, a voice called out: "Abimelch forty-eight all out! Ishmael one hundred and eleven for six! Well played Peterson!"

Oh fuck, Keith recognised the source of the scene's dread.

The master took the captain's hand and shook it. The jubilant Ishmaelis patted backs and whooped as the Abimelchians sloped off back to the changing rooms in grass-streaked silence.

The match had been on Top-Field due to the sorry state of the cricket oval, which had suffered irreparable damage during the ignominy of the end of term fête. Hundreds of people and dozens of tents mercilessly raped its three-hundred-year old lawn.

"You fucking twat, Keith!" a young Ben called out. "At least give us some sport when we crush you!"

Keith endured the long walk back down to the school; even his own team was hanging back, joining the abuse.

"My grandmother could have caught that lob!" one of his teammates shouted.

"Piss off, Whinstone! If you hadn't bowled like a complete flid, they might not have been smacking sixes off us for the last hour and a half."

"Ha! Remember that? We killed you, right?"

"Sorry… what?" It took Keith a few seconds to snap back to the present.

The cricketing clip had probably been captured by a kid with a phone. It had paused again, returning to its picturesque freeze frame. Keith's mind had skipped on a few chapters as a succession of memories from Gladworth's, triggered by the video, played within his mind.

"We slaughtered you!"

"Yep, don't think I played my best that day."

"I got the vid from Hendy. Remember him? He was in your house, wasn't he?"

"Er, yeah. Dark hair, big farter?"

"Christ yes, he was a colossal farter wasn't he! Yes, he works for my father now. He dug out a bunch of stuff back from the old school. I'll ping them over to you if you like."

"Sounds great. I'd somehow forgotten how much fun we had," Keith said.

Ben either missed the sarcasm or let it slip. "So you've decided to swallow your pride and take me up on the offer to come and work for us?"

After Uni, Keith had tried to find a job to fit his aspirations. Any residual optimism had been abraded by four years of shitty minimum wage jobs in the sham economy. Unemployment for under thirties was forty-two per cent, official inflation was fourteen per cent, while prospects for improvement were negligible. The desperate faces of the people on the streets gave a more accurate picture than any government numbers. He knew the despair of the people. He was intimately acquainted with it. His pride, by now, was only a small mouthful; so yes, he would swallow it. It was either that or join the army, which was always ravenous for young men with limited options.

There was a polite knock at the door and the pretty receptionist entered again, this time carrying a wooden tray with two cups of coffee, sugar, and biscuits. Two small, stainless steel jugs of milk also sat on the tray. One was beaded in condensation; the other was steaming gently. The smell arrived a few seconds later. The volatile perfumed tang insinuated itself into Keith's nasal epithelial tissue and raced on into his mind. The quality of the experience had nothing in common with the coffee-flavoured drinks found on the high street.

The tray was presented first to Keith, the guest. He took a cup and poured in a little of the hot milk, dropped in one lumpy brown crystal of cane sugar, and took a tiny silver spoon. He smiled his acceptance and the receptionist straightened out of her bow, turned to Ben and repeated the ceremony. Ben took a handful of biscuits, a good long look at her cleavage, and his coffee black.

Once they were alone again, Ben continued. "The world's a mess, people are pissed off, while at the same time there's a mint to be made!"

"A mint? I would be happy to start off with a fraction of a mint and work my way up," Keith joked. "I could start at the bottom. I don't need any special favours."

Ben looked directly at Keith, at the coffee, and back to Keith's cheap shoes and suit. He didn't have to say anything. They both knew he had been granted a special favour just to be sitting in this office. Ben pulled a printout from the desk and shook it at Keith.

"Not easy to put you in a pigeon hole, though. Warehouse experience, barista, pest control…"

Keith hated his CV.

***

On the platform again, he was now acutely aware of the greasy, gritty warm air blowing around his ears. By the time he arrived home, his face and hands and the phlegm from his lungs would all be streaked with black. But it was not

London's physical filth that made him feel dirty.

At the age of eleven, through some strange quirk of fate and bureaucracy, and to the astonishment and outrage of his bullies, Keith had been whisked away from the casual institutionalised belligerence of state care. He was given, what had been described at the time as, a life of privilege. Even the young Keith was old enough to know that getting a scholarship to an elite school would eventually make the difference between stacking shelves and earning stacks of cash. On a day-to-day basis, the only difference had been the bullies' accents and the disappointing inversion of the cabbage to chip ratio at meal times.

The school he and Ben had attended catered for the children of the one per cent. It unquestionably delivered a five-star education. Yet, despite astronomical fees and almost scandalous profitability, the amenities were two star at best; apparently, discomfort was an integral part of the approach, which also featured plenty of physical exercise, institutionalised bullying, and austere meals.

Ben had belonged there. His father was one of Britain's cabal of oligarchs. His company—now Keith's company too, he realised with a shudder of revulsion—had fingers in too many pies to count. Again, Keith was one of the token poor people. Over the years, his naive incomprehension at the source of the distinction between him and the other boys had been replaced with a rigid belief in his own moral superiority. He was real. He came up from the bottom, and he appreciated the worth of privilege and money. He had been convinced that, one day, he would go into the world and make it a better place.

Inside and out, he felt dirty with the new BHJ corporate card itching through his thin polyester trouser pocket. He pushed in his ear buds and tuned in to the big screen, which seemed to show a different portion of the same programme he had caught earlier. At least, it was the same reporter who had been swimming and chatting with the dolphin.

A voice was talking over a collage of disturbing images, featuring lots of monkeys in cages:

Europe had gotten the ball rolling, in 2005, with the great-apes. Twenty years later, 'human' rights belonged to five species other than Homo sapiens. But the fight is not over. Victims of cruelty and slavery, who can't communicate their suffering or make their own demands, are too easily ignored. Now we have a strange catch twenty-two, with the recognition as people proving to be a two-edged sword. The REVOBS laws can't apply to people, so unlike the honeybees or mosquitoes, nobody represents the sentient. Without their own voice, they have been stuck in limbo, until now…

The screen was showing a sequence of unpleasant photo-graphs and clips: animals with wires sewn into their shaved scalps; robot arms wired into primate brains; brain-scan-ning bath-caps fitted to dolphins; animations showing images retrieved and loaded into cat optic nerves; finally, cute pictures of baby dolphins and chimps playing with baby humans.

With each little step, we learnt more and, eventually, we learnt to read their minds! We scanned their brains to get at their thoughts. Symbols translated to and from our own languages.

More pictures of baby animals.

We learnt how to miniaturise brain-scanning equipment.
We could finally talk to each other.

The screen suddenly filled with the frenetic 'GNN Special' animation. Keith and the other viewers on the platform were invited to explore the science behind the miracle.

White lab coats paraded in front of backdrops of fantastically complex lab equipment. As a prelude, a woman with "locked-in syndrome" talked to Barry, using the same technology. She explained in her own voice, synthesised from old home movies, how voices and even pictures could be sent straight into her brain and words and images plucked back out. Barry asked her to picture him, and a hilarious big nosed homunculus was extracted from amongst the noise of a hundred billion neurons and shared for the merriment of the audience.

A train had come and gone. It had been too full as usual. Keith could probably have fought his way onto it, but the GNN preview was fascinating enough that he didn't mind. He would try to stream the programme it was advertising once he got home.

He was surprised to find it was already dark when he emerged from the subterranean microclimate. It was also bloody cold. He trudged through the black streets, walked under dead or flickering streetlights, and avoided anoraked gangs of youths on the corners. He watched life projected in silhouette onto bedsit curtains. He bought a *kebap* at the shop below his room and ate it at the counter facing the street. It was warmer there than inside his flat.

Outside, steam rose from a manhole. A man ran by, looking back over his shoulder. A girl in a yellow dress—with far too much bared and bluing skin showing—blew him a kiss through the window when he caught her eyeing his *kebap*.

He chucked the greasy paper in the bin and headed up the corridor by the side of the shop. He squeezed past stacks of boxes full of dehydrated chips. He climbed up the stairs to his room and walked past the shared bathroom, with its plughole stuffed with clotted soap and dreadlocks. He took out his keys and let himself in, took a piss at the sink, sloshing the splashes of yellow urine down with water from a chipped cup.

Sink, sofa bed, hotplate, fridge, and window. The fridge contained a can of beer. Keith grabbed it and collapsed into the brown frayed armchair, turning on his screen and flicking past the few messages waiting.

```
Msg: Shaun [@Schaun2Twefford, Junior Manager BHJ Plc, no
relationship status, no additional details added] has
requested you add him back as a friend.

Msg: Subject: Your Country Needs You! Enlist! [The world
is a dangerous place…]

Msg: Subject: Welcome Day Badge ID [Dear Keith, welcome
to BHJ…]
```

Dismissing the notifications, he scrolled directly to 'The Smiths', an inane police procedural that was one of his guilty pleasures. The flashy, sexy credits rolled, and he popped open the can.

When the main event arrived, Barry tried to keep the conversation light, focusing on the wonder of the technology that allowed such a touching of minds so alien. He compared the meeting to Da Vinci's 'Hand of God.' He asked about breath-holding, fish, the dolphin's relationship to Jesus. At this point, an abrupt translation error in the mechanical voice of the computer informed the viewers that the concept had not survived mimetic conversion.

Blue, his guest, lolling in a big tank surrounded by armed police and more wires and bulky equipment than was strictly necessary, would not stay on safe, cosy topics. Symbols plucked from his brain were transformed into words and spoken to millions of live viewers. He urged the people of Nippon to recognise him as a person and to free him from the solitary confinement he had suffered since the abduction of his mother and sister. He denied being the leader of Nebulous, the notorious eco-insurgents.

His synthesised, but sonorous, voice read sections of his book, spending minutes complaining about oil slicks, dead zones, and an ocean full of plastic flakes. It asked us to stop destroying the planet and killing his folk. It spoke of his wish for freedom, how he longed to swim beneath the vast undulating mirror of the ocean, dive into darkness, chase and herd balls of chaotic flashing fish, rather than chomping down the stiff dead food flung daily into his pool, of his desire for sex—most of which had to be bleeped out when his lyrical prose became a little too enthusiastic about the desire to chase, exhaust, and penetrate some smooth-skinned cow...

The audience was shocked and spellbound. It might have

been the zeitgeist, though it was just as likely Ralph Moody's digitised voice issuing from Blue's speech synthesiser; the star's deep timbre empowering the words with a mystical aura of persuasion. Whatever the fundamental reason for the sociological resonance, the world went wild. People, exhausted from the years of collapse and perpetually disappointed by ever remote promises of recovery, grabbed hold of the issue, like drowning men clutching at a dangling shoelace. Action was demanded. Blue's bobbing head, with its enlightened smile and scathing words, didn't just go viral; it spread around the world like a pandemic. His mostly ghost-written autobiography became the most downloaded book of all time.

Two years after the first famous interview had been broadcast, Barry was again dominating the world's screens, promoting amongst a throng of opportunistic celebrities outside the UN, while the historic vote was taken.

Yehan Munisai put down his Companion and turned off the TV, which was still broadcasting the gushing analysis of the event and showing jubilant scenes from outside the General Assembly building in Jerusalem. Almost unanimously, with the notable exception of Nippon, the delegates had recognised Cetaceans as people and brought them under the protection of the Universal Declaration of Human Rights. In this acknowledgement, they became one with the orangutans, bonobos, gorillas, and chimps. Of course, the declaration wasn't what it might once have been. The world and the seas were pretty much fucked by then, anyway.

The old man took off his glasses and dabbed at his eyes with a tissue. He turned to the window and, blinking the moisture away, looked out at the hills and buildings of Uwajima. Beyond it all: the sea! This was the sea that had made his family so astonishingly rich. He wanted to go down to the sea again, just like he had as a child. He wanted to roll up his trousers and let the cool water wash the sand from between his toes. But he couldn't, not right now—instead, with a bamboo stylus, he wrote a letter to his lawyer, recorded a statement to his notepad, and made his longhaired waster grandson the 56th richest man in the world. Niato, the radical who had brought so much shame on their family with his stunts and who had been right all along!

The tuna farms, fish markets, canning plants, and sushi

chain, with its twenty thousand restaurants worldwide, were all now his. Yehan's children would be furious, murderous even, as would hundreds of assorted nephews and nieces, but it had to be done; the stain needed to be wiped away.

Yehan sat, nearly motionless, as he suffered the ache from his back and legs. He waited for his lawyer to send back the confirmation that the transfer was legal. Then, he pushed himself to his feet and shuffled on stiff legs over to the shrine devoted to the family's patron, his own great-grandfather, who had fought against the Americans with the swords that rested below his portrait. Yehan had never studied the fighting arts; but, burning with shame, while reading the dolphin's book for the third time, he had planned for this moment. He took the smaller of the two swords in his left hand and slowly settled his old body down onto the floor by the window. While making sure he could still see the sea, he lay the sword across his lap. The wood was hard and his joints were already complaining.

He knew they called him the King of the Sea. Once, seemingly in another time, a younger and more brazen version of himself had found the title amusing, happily tolerating the endearing jest. Now, he saw it as a badge of shame. A king had responsibilities, and he had ignored them all. Now he only hoped that, if history remembered their name, it would be for the great works of his grandson, not for the crimes of his ancestor.

He pulled the small gun, that had also belonged to his great-grandfather, out of its cloth bag and took its barrel into his mouth, where it rested on his tongue like a cold cock.

He prayed one last time to his ancestors that his grandson

would do the right thing, and then pulled the trigger.

***

Niato Munisai had never been the rich kid who protested his hatred for money, while accepting its help in insulating him from the daily travails of life. He had grown up with his mother's tales of the sea and loved the living things it contained. But, when he looked at the world with his own eyes, he realised these were stories from another time. The real ocean, away from their private beach, was a filthy puddle, and his family had helped make it that way.

When the news of his grandfather's death reached him, he was with a small team of bearded vegetarians creeping around Macau's vast docks. They lurked in the shadows amongst the cyclopean machines, avoiding surveillance while snarling the propellers of container ships with bundles of carbon nano-fibres.

When he was a teenager, his grandfather had been infuriated by the boy's inflexible moral position. They had argued about the life choices he was making. He had accused the patriarch of theft, of wantonly raiding and despoiling the ocean commons that were the birth right of every citizen of earth. After he was cast out, only his mother, who had always been quietly proud of his stand, had kept in touch.

Niato stopped short when he read the subject of the alert off his wrist. He immediately found somewhere, out of sight, to listen to the message. Attached to the message was a photograph of a letter his grandfather had left for him.

With a flash, a memory asserted itself. He remembered

clutching the old man's bony hands with his own chubby, short fingers, the sand cold and wet under his bare feet as he shrieked with some combination of terror and elation. Then they had both scampered back from a wave that threatened to soak their trousers. He had loved his grandfather. Now he was gone, and there was no longer anything to prove.

As he read its simple stark lines, he wept, just as he had all those years ago while driving away from the abandoned Blue.

He had slipped into a trance, was mentally somewhere else. He couldn't consciously hear the shouted warnings and could not respond to the increasingly frantic calls of his Companion.

He was taken by surprise when four security guards suddenly lurched around the corner in front of him, while another pair had simultaneously snuck up behind. He fought like crazy. He fought them as if they were personally responsible for the pollution, the killing and, most of all, for the death of his grandfather. He fought, despite being shot twice with electro-darts. He finally fell when the pepper spray and choke holds of the guards made it impossible for him to breathe.

When he woke, he was slumped against a rusty orange shipping container, with his hands tightly cable-tied behind his back. His eyes and face burnt, as if they had been plunged into a boiling pot, and his nose and throat were half-clogged with phlegm and vomit. Four security guards eyed him warily; one, clearly injured in the scuffle, was holding a bloody tissue to his nose.

Somehow, despite everything, the family muddled through, prospered even. The boys grew up quickly. In the autumn, they harvested apples and wild mushrooms and spent the summers fishing from the banks of the Rheine, which hadn't been as clean and teaming with fish for a hundred years. Winters were harsh, though. Fuel was expensive when bought legally from government depots, which were a joke anyway. The long, slow-burn war with the Caliph and the constant niggling of domestic terrorism ensured there was never enough to go around. The black market always seemed to have enough, but their prices targeted the rich with their minimalist Swedish ovens and fake coal fires. 'Slum dwellers' foraged for scraps of wood or hacked branches off the city's diminishing number of trees.

The inhabitants of the old print building, at 43 Henkelkai, were well-to-do amongst the down-at-heel. This made them a target. To rob the rich, you needed hacking skills to get past security systems and drones to peer over walls. This level of sophistication was out of reach for most casual criminals and thugs. Their only option was to rob from the poor; a handful of eggs or a couple of glitchy Companions would do for a night's work. With little police presence, subtlety was not a necessity, and the people who had found their vocation rioting and smashing things, now applied their new skills to less politically motivated unrest.

Anosh had never been a great fan of violence. He used to play shooters as a kid; and, once in a while, back when he had a job, an office colleague might initiate a birthday party paintball outing. This was poor preparation for prolonged apocalypse survival; but, having recognised this, for the last three weeks, he had been taking a shotgun on trips to the woods where he would line up and shoot down cans.

Lying awake on several consecutive nights, he debated with internal voices. There was a difference between cans and people; but he decided, if he ever needed to choose between his family and a violent mob, he would not hesitate to pull the trigger.

The top stories of Maslow's pyramid-of-needs eroded away terrifyingly quickly. Humans were passably civilised when resources were plentiful, but the amygdala switched on primal and unsavoury programming when things got tight.

***

Their little boat, a small sailing dinghy that Anosh and Vikram had repaired, hugged the bank on the inside of a long meander. Its progress was slow against the current. The banks of the great river were scattered with fishermen and sunbathers, enjoying what might prove to be the last of the year's clement weather. Ayşe lay with her back to the stern, propped up on a pile of cushions, finally finding the chance to finish the book that had absorbed her for the past week.

A cold, salty wind was blowing down from Denmark, but the sky was clear and the sun hot. They set off early, with Anosh herding the kids out of the house before the perfect sailing weather blew itself out. If the wind held until lunchtime, they would make the seven kilometres upriver to the little wood, where they hoped to fill their baskets with autumn mushrooms. On the way back, they could furl the sails and let the current carry them home.

The boys would take turns at the tiller and keep the boat pointed towards the slower water, near the banks. Anosh would work the sails and call directions. Zaki was reading their progress off a battered old Companion that Anosh had patched up for him. There were millions of obsolete phones and tablets in circulation. After a little tinkering and the installation of one of the open source OSs, most could be coaxed back into service. He had given the battered old thing to Zaki for his thirteenth birthday.

"When are we there?" asked Siegfried.

"Not long," muttered Ayşe, looking up from her book. "Anosh, you have to read this after me."

"Is it really written by a fish, Mami?"

"He's a dolphin, darling, and dolphins are not fish."

"Siegfried, I've told you that before," Anosh interrupted, slightly exasperated. He felt hostile to anything too popular. "It's probably just a ghost-written gimmick, anyway."

"I don't think so," said Ayşe, "and if it is, the author deserves a prize!"

"Careful, Segi! Don't steer us out into the current!"

The younger boy, only eleven and, to his annoyance, still treated like a baby by his parents, tugged on the tiller and guided the boat back towards the bank. A big barge was coming towards them, and he had become distracted looking at the bandoliered security crew leaning over the railings at the front.

"Nearly there!" Zaki shouted, twenty minutes later. Anosh took the Companion and checked they really were at their destination. He dropped the sails and ran the little dinghy gently into the bank, where Zaki jumped off with the line and fastened it to a small tree.

"Good boy! That's a nice bowline."

Siegfried hopped to shore next, and then held out his hand to help his mum. Anosh and Ayşe exchanged an indulgent smile as they watched this display of chivalry.

They all spent the next few hours in the woods, hunting for mushrooms. The boys dug under bushes and pushed through dense undergrowth to outdo each other with size and number. They used a cached Meshpedia article on the Companion to check that their booty was not poisonous, and Ayşe double-checked before letting anything into her basket. She had collected mushrooms with her grandmother as a young girl, but she still needed to look up many of the unfamiliar European specimens. They gathered a good-sized haul, enough for a week of omelettes.

The wood was relatively remote, and they had arrived early on the first sunny day for a week. For two hours they didn't meet another soul. Once they had exhausted the fungal resources in the immediate area, Anosh set up some bottles and fir cones on a spongy stump and backed off twenty metres. He made the boys stay behind him with their mother. He insisted they plug their ears. He was never excessive with ammunition, because it was so difficult to get hold of shells, but he needed the confidence to load, aim, and fire and wanted to feel familiar with these skills if he ever needed to rely on reflexes in a tight situation.

Zaki was allowed to fire both barrels and was thrilled to hit his dirty green wine bottle target. Anosh wanted to offer the loaded weapon to Segi, but Ayşe glared at him. After a few more shots and more shredded foliage, they packed up and headed back to the boat. They took a different loop in the path, hoping to find blackberries or opportunistic 'bush tucker', but the forest animals were either keeping a low profile or already eaten.

They were rounding a bend in the path, when they heard voices approaching. Anosh signalled to Ayşe. She knew the drill and quickly hid most of their loot in her rucksack, leaving just a few poor specimens in the bottom of a conspicuously empty basket.

After a few minutes listening to the approaching commotion, they saw a large group of scruffy Camp Kids tramping between the trees. They all carried stout sticks, and a couple had nasty-looking catapults. The oldest was probably about eighteen and the youngest looked to be about six, but he could just as well be an undernourished ten. They stopped when they saw the family. Anosh continued walking, trying to look friendly and unthreatening. The oldest boy hesitated a few seconds and then spat, aggressively, in his path. The large, snotty ball of phlegm was taken as a signal by his chums, and they spread out to block the way.

Zaki looked to his dad; Siegfried froze, clutching onto his mother's hand. Ayşe put her hand to the scarf at her waist, where she kept the little 3D-printed, single-use, four-shooter that Anosh made her carry whenever they went into the 'wilderness'.

Neither party made a move. When the stand-off began to feel uncomfortable, Anosh casually undid a button on the shotgun's sling, causing it to swing from beside his rucksack into a horizontal position. He didn't make eye contact with any of the older boys; he didn't want this to be about honour or pride where things could get quickly out of hand. He just looked about the forest and let his hand rest on top of his gun's barrel. As the group eyed the sleek, minimalist, matte black device, a little afternoon menacing was beginning to look less appealing.

Even without a signal from their leader, the kids spontaneously drifted off into the trees. Sensing he had lost the initiative, the big kid turned and followed his gang without a noise.

The tension was broken. Siegfried burst into tears.

Anosh tussled his son's hair and told him not to worry. "The silly boys are gone again."

"I wasn't scared!" boasted Zaki.

"There is nothing wrong with being a bit scared; it stops you from being silly!" Anosh told him.

When they got back to where they had moored up, they found that, where frontal assault had failed, the gang had resorted to asymmetric tactics. The boat was gone, its cut line still fastened to the tree. They could see it floating away with the current, a few hundred metres downriver. Anosh cursed. He was tempted to hunt down the little shits.

The journey back took the rest of the day, and it was getting dark before they got home. The next few weeks were wet and windy, and then winter started, with early snows and weeks of freezing rain.

***

When it had become clear to everyone that the wheels had finally come off the world, Anosh's first reaction had been relief. Finally, the charade was over, and he felt vindicated after years of telling anybody who would listen that there was no endgame plan for a society with such massive debt and inequality. For a while, bolstered by righteousness, he had felt that optimism might be warranted. Perhaps, now that everybody accepted there was a problem, things could be sorted out; healing could begin. It was obviously not fair for the top one per cent to get everything, and now people would finally work together to build a better world.

Early on, it looked like optimism might prevail. Enthusiastic clubs of like-minded people had sprung up. They built windmills and set up rooftop solar farms; people planted tomatoes and cabbages in window boxes. Unfortunately, for every productive new age tinker hippie, there were a hundred confused, desperate, hungry citizens. They queued for handouts or clustered after hours for warmth in schools and sports centres. The blackouts and food shortages, with unemployment peaking at sixty per cent, pushed great blocks of people over the edge, forcing them into dependence on a state that could barely keep the rubbish out of the streets or pay for heating in the hospitals.

Way Forward parties spread across Europe, shamelessly exploiting the fear and ignorance at the bottom to justify crackdowns and policies—which, disappointingly, to Anosh at least, seemed designed to benefit only those at the top.

In the affluent suburbs, spikes were added to walls, and gated neighbourhoods of MacMansions were patrolled by security drones. Within these homes, people's lives carried on mostly unchanged. Executives tele-commuted via corporate satellite uplink or crunched along the pitted tarmac with their 'eco-hybrid SUVs'. The poor had to fend for themselves, while the privileged continued to be paid via loophole tunnelling shell companies.

The government did its bit. Judicious troop deployments kept a semblance of law and order and, at first, holes in the road were small enough to be an inconvenience, rather than a danger.

Slowly, though, as the shelves had run out of food and the heating had failed, the abdication of personal responsibility escalated. An unwieldly mass of people had grown up expecting an unending supply of chicken nuggets. They had been reassured by ad saturated broadcasting that this was not only okay, but it was their right. Now their world view was being annihilated and they had no chance to adjust. Life got increasingly bitter, and even the optimists eventually learnt that when the going gets tough…
…people turn into monsters.

Anosh killed his first human being in December of 2027.

For weeks, the situation had been gaining in intensity. Racial pretexts, fanned by Forward rhetoric, were used to justify an escalating campaign of attacks and robberies. Despite all the hate shouted from street corners or parks, deep down it was about food and power, not skin colour or religion. The Sikhs downstairs were a visible minority. For the proto-tribes forming on the streets, their brown skin, turbans, and possession of food made them a target. During the 'shortages' the exotic smells escaping the Sikhs' kitchen were taken as an incitement to riot. The mob got it into their heads they must have some secret stash. Anosh and Ayşe had once joked about the same thing in awe of this ability to synthesise a gourmet experience from the simplest ingredients. In the house, the families often shared what little they could scrabble together. Segi would take down a bag of potatoes or a bunch of onions and, later, when a kid had thundered up the stairs to deliver a bowl of aromatic magic, they would all wonder at the transformation.

Anosh was up on the roof, manually aligning the solar panels. Below on the street, a bunch of youths and opportunistic troublemakers rollicked and capered. They were rolling a burning tire ahead of them and casually flinging stones at any unbroken panes of glass they spotted. The heavy, angry rioting of the early years had taken place mainly in the city centres. Few street-level windows survived, and the cars left parked or abandoned were universally rolled or burnt out. The destruction in the surrounding zones had been less complete, but that just meant there was still fuel to attract the frustrated, confused packs, whose daily routine consisted of undirected destruction.

People kept back from windows or watched from the roofs as the gang passed. As they entered the great cloud of garlic and spice-flavoured steam spilling from the Sikhs' kitchen window, they paused like hounds catching a scent. As he watched from the roof, Anosh saw their casual recreational vandalism had become focused. A premonition sent him dashing to the stairs.

There was no logic; a survival programme, 'out group aggression', had been initiated and, without conscious communication, the gang had an enemy.

They were hungry and the Pakis were clearly taking the piss, a good brick through the window and a bit of looting would sort out the smug bastards.

Anosh had learnt a lot about his Sikh housemates over the past couple of years. They were complex and proud, a people with a history littered with massacres, expulsions, and war. To Anosh, it was clear that the women ran the show. The kids were happy and respectful. The men wore turbans and carried Kirpans, which were at least as serviceable as they were ceremonial.

At first, the two families living on the bottom floors had kept to themselves. They chatted and were polite, but Anosh and his family were not part of their clan. Over the years, though, as things had become increasingly tough, that was changing. 43 Henkelkai had become their castle, and all the families had adopted the shared goal of not allowing their members to be harmed or their food and possessions stolen.

A raucous chanting broke out. Dustbin lids were beaten, stones flung, and a chunk of concrete the size of a grapefruit left the centre of the skirmishers. It arced through the frigid air before crashing through the papered-over glass panel in the kitchen door. There was a moment of silence and then a jeer went up from the street.

The raucous chanting had barely gotten going, when a mass of screaming men in turbans sprinted from the house. The steel of weapons flashed. To the thugs, it was as if they had appeared from another century. The mob hadn't done their research when they attacked a heavily armed group of warrior saints.

A quick, but vicious, skirmish ended with some nasty bleeding wounds and a few severed fingers that lay amongst the confusion of bloody footprints. The energy of the initial clash ebbed and the two sides drew apart, facing off and screaming abuse, while assessing the damage. Vikram, the doctor and head of the family, raised his sabre again and cried something foreign and threatening, then his sons took up the cry. They lifted their arms and pointed weapons towards a spotless white sky. The rioters, unused to organised retaliation, and shocked by the effectiveness of the long, curving swords and daggers, spontaneously broke and dashed, or limped, back the way they had come. One of the fleeing wounded only made it two steps, before collapsing in the snow, horrible sucking whistling sounds coming from beneath his jacket. The Sikhs watched the pack scatter up the road and vanish into side streets.

Vikram handed his sword to his oldest son and squatted next to the terrified kid, who, without the mask of rage twisting his face, looked to be about seventeen. The youth looked back, his face ashen, his eyes desperate and pleading.

 "He's got a punctured lung, let's get him inside!"

"What?! This *Arschloch* tried to kill us!" screamed one of the older boys. A stare from his father was enough; together, they heaved the dying boy inside and out of the cold.

Anosh had raced down the stairs from the roof to warn Ayşe of the trouble. They had watched the commotion from an upstairs window. When Ayşe saw the kid being carried inside, she went down to help, while Anosh stayed for a few minutes keeping watch to make sure no reinforcements were on their way.

The boy was laid on a kitchen table and his clothes ripped open. A whistling sound and a nasty frothing bubbling came from a five-centimetre gash on his side. By now, his lungs were filling with blood. His lips were becoming blue, his face ashen. Air filling the space beneath his ribs was collapsing his lungs and slowly suffocating him.

At Vikram's instruction, Ayşe pressed a damp cloth to the gash.

"That should stop more air getting in," Vikram said, while he fiddled with a pen.

Anosh watched as the doctor dismantled it, emptied and discarded the inside, leaving only the tube. This he quickly passed to his wife.

"Sterilise this as best you can, please."

While she was washing the pen, Vikram cut one finger from a surgical glove and removed its fingertip to make a floppy latex tube open at both ends. The patient was getting noticeably bluer. Vikram took the gutted pen and threaded it through the hole in the glove's severed finger. It flopped about on the end of the pen like some kid's cute novelty eraser. Vikram fastened it tightly in place with an

122

elastic band, turned to the youth and placed a hand on his forehead.

"This will hurt, but don't worry; it's going to save your life."

Ayşe removed her bloody cloth and Anosh was horrified to see the doctor gently slide the pen into the wound. The kid writhed in pain. Anosh and one of Vikram's sons rushed forward to restrain him. Vikram explored the wound with the tip of the pen. This was excruciating, but mercifully the kid didn't have enough air to scream, and his struggles quickly ran out of energy. He twitched for a while and finally passed out as the pain and shock overcame him.

After more poking around inside the boy's chest, there was a sudden rush of air, which made a farting sound as it passed through the pen tube and out through the severed finger of the rubber glove. Now, when the boy breathed in, the rubber tube sucked shut, serving as a crude, but effective, valve. Vikram packed the cloth around the pen to make a seal, and they watched as the valve and the boy's own breathing siphoned off the remaining air. The rhythm of his breathing quickly improved and soon his lips regained colour.

The next half hour was less intense, but no less hectic, as Vikram's wife sewed up the gash. They smeared the wound with Vaseline and bandaged it with a damp cloth to make a seal and to prevent any more air from getting in. The kid woke up and passed out several more times before the job was finished. When they finally stepped back, Vikram said a little prayer of thanks, and then went to wash his hands and change out of his bloody clothes.

Humans seemed instinctively to understand the power politics of the new reality; after all, they evolved with it. Organisational units of more than a few dozen people were a recent graft onto a much older behavioural tree. The rules of kings and priests and governments must be taught, but all are born knowing the rules of clan altruism and the dance of tribal war.

With collapse, the emerging communes, with their roof gardens and self-sufficiency manifesto, fell into the role of settled, peaceful farmers. The mobs were the raiders. When a village stood up and fought back, repelling the attack, it was an existential moment for those whose instincts had assigned them the survival strategy of thievery and murder. Face would be lost, the crucial fear factor diminished, and bullying would become unprofitable.

What was an out of work thug turned security guard or an unemployed part-time football hooligan to do? Should the neo-Nazi plasterer plant potatoes on his mother's front garden? There were no decisions or discussions. Civilisation was suspended; behaviour half a million years old reasserted itself.

The battle wasn't over; the thugs were always going to come back and finish the job. Anosh and Vikram had known this, even if their wives hoped otherwise.

***

Two-week-old snow covered the streets of the old docks. It lay piled against walls or compacted down to grey ice by passing people and vehicles. The smell of wood smoke and the odd frozen lump of yellow horseshit gave the city a Dickensian aspect. This was only added to by the increasing number of refugees. Anosh and Ayşe were up on the roof wearing anoraks. He was watching the street as she finished making the last of the signs she had insisted they hang around their building.

Bewaffnet Verteidigung! Armed Response!

"I still think they will just see it as a challenge," he criticised.

"If we are going to have to shoot people, I want it to be a last resort, and I want to warn them first," said Ayşe.

They had eaten dinner, their own sun-dried tomatoes and pasta from the store rations. It was cold, but clear outside. Anosh had decided to sit for a while up on the roof, a thick blanket pulled up over his dressing gown. He listened to the sounds of the town, alert for signs of trouble.

He had planned to join Ayşe in bed, but must have fallen asleep while looking up at the stars, because he woke up with freezing, sweaty spit coating the side of his face. His entire body was icy cold. It was 11.30 pm, and he had been asleep for an hour. He grabbed the door handle to let himself back in; it was icy against his fingers.

In the stairwell, it was quiet with a faint snoring coming from somebody on the second floor. Some super-power sense made him look out of the stair window, and he made out half a dozen dark shapes, creeping along the street. As he watched, they huddled to the side. He had to lean forward, gently pressing his forehead against the glass to continue his spying. Smoke drifted from a clasped object. Flames flashed, sending shadows dancing onto the snow.

One of the mob approached the building, a determined set to his stride. Anosh, still groggy, only belatedly realised what was happening. It was too late to wake the others. Now, in a panic, he dashed down the stairs two at a time. He reached the cabinet, in what had once been a broom cupboard, and unlocked it with the small key he always kept on him. He fumbled around inside. His fingers found the metal of the patiently waiting shotgun.

A dancing light was casting shadows towards him. He saw a dark shape holding the Molotov cocktail—for that was clearly what it was—stalking up the street towards their home. Upstairs and through the doors behind him, two dozen people slept helplessly. Anosh imagined the carnage and inferno that would follow if the shadow drew back his arm and threw the bottle.

He quietly unlocked the door and then slammed it open. The thug was barely six metres away. He froze in surprise, mid-throw, arm back, yellow flames and oily smoke twisting away from the cloth rammed into the bottle's neck. The thug took in the raised shotgun. Eyes met. Time was frozen. Something passed between them, something very old.

Flash! Bang! A blade of flame sprang from the first barrel; it clipped the thug, erasing an ear and taking an apple-sized chunk out of the side of his head.

Flash! Bang! The second barrel took him in the neck and upper chest. The mangled body began a backflip, which was stopped short by the ground. The body collapsed into a rag doll heap, squirting blood onto the snow; arms and legs splayed at unnatural angles. Two seconds of frozen time later, the bottle exploded with a small whoosh, and the body was cloaked by flame and smoke.

Through the fire, Anosh watched the backs of the other black shapes running away. His ears were ringing. He imagined the shots still echoing through the empty streets. Vikram had appeared. He grabbed Anosh by the arm and dragged him back into the house.

Anosh noticed they were both wearing pyjamas, socked feet melting the snow.

"You'll get wet feet," Anosh pointed out.

"Good grief, never mind that," said Vikram. "We have got to get you off the street. Quick. And stop waving the gun around. Hopefully nobody has seen you yet."

Back inside, Anosh leant the gun next to the radiator. Self had been disengaged, while autopilot had acted; but now, his mind was integrating the responsibility and repercussions of the autopilot's actions back into his own narrative. He began to shake and found he needed to sit down.

He looked up from the seated fetal position his body had chosen, to see the two older sons of the family from the second floor hurrying down the stairs. They were dressed in black; hoodies up over their heads, drawn in tight to hide their faces. They nodded at Vikram and Anosh and then left the kitchen through a side door.

Over the weeks since the first attack, the men had discussed various scenarios. They had kept things simple, but there were two strict principles: the shotgun would always be ready, and any bodies would be immediately dumped in the river. The old warehouse building backed onto a narrow canal, but they had decided it would be better to go another hundred metres to the end of the quay, where the canal met the river. There, the current should carry away any evidence.

The two boys left through a back door to slip around to the front of the house. They would wrap the body in a sheet and, if they had time, scoop the bloody snow into bin bags.

No words were spoken when the body was tossed into the oily black water. It sank and then, caught by the current, surfaced metres away, as just another indistinct shape floating towards the sea:

Dangling arms and legs are blindly grasping tentacles hanging below its bin-bag body. A necrotic jelly fish, kept afloat by a trapped last breath forced from dead lungs by the drop into the silent cold water.

Geography was becoming irrelevant. Pieces of Third World embedded themselves in the First. Billionaires built en-claves, wherever whim dictated. The concept of country began to sound quaint. Old geopolitical maps, with their pinks and greens, began to writhe and flow obscenely; free trade zones and jurisdictional satellites thrust pseudopods and vesicles of experimental government into each other. Great gulps of ocean were squatted as quasi-national au-tonomous marine areas.

Stella woke to the sounds of the market. They had been learning about the new Caliph's empire in school, and she had been dreaming of flying carpets and palaces with onion-shaped domes and evil scheming Grand Viziers. The pots and pans, fish and fruit in the market below would have been familiar to Aladdin. Other trinkets, Spex or Companions, would have been coveted as wondrous magical artefacts, able to invoke illusions or cast sight into the ocean below, even allowing the wielder to peer through the eyes of fabulous creatures.

The voices and cries were filtered and stretched as they resonated within the big feed drum. She lay for a few minutes, getting a feel for the mood, then she struggled into her jeans and did her best to brush the knots out of her jet-black hair. She pushed open the hanging door and confidently clambered down the netting to the pontoon.

After the blue glow of the drum, it took her eyes several minutes to recalibrate their white balance and bleach the orange stain from the world.

When she eventually found him, Marcel was furtively grilling a stack of squid on the small fire he had made at the bottom of a flight of stairs leading down to the water. He was careful to keep them turning fast to avoid burning the pale flesh. A bigger fire would be better, but that would draw too much attention. Marcel had already tried to scrounge a place at one of the regular spots, but having grown into a spotty youth, he wasn't tolerated to the same extent he had been as a scruffy little boy. It was unlikely people would accept the intrusion and inevitable fishy smell.

"Hi Stella," he said as she walked over.

"Hi, Manu."

"You want to help me sell these?" he asked smiling, knowing the crew of the Reefer was much more likely to buy from a pretty girl and much less likely to haggle.

"Fifty cents each, okay? Seventy-five for the big one with the long legs," he said.

"Okay, half for me?"

"Yeah, all right," he reluctantly agreed, certain he was being blatantly exploited. "Tell them I've got some blue crabs, too."

He gestured towards a net bag tied at the bottom of the steps, just under the water.

"There are loads of them in the weed, under the service skiff ramp."

"Cool."

Stella wrapped the crispy squid in some sheets of paper that Marcel must have snatched from the office shredder chute. Operational security was not a concept the kids were familiar with, but many skippers were just as interested in the titbits of industrial espionage printed on the wrapping as they were with the tasty grilled seafood inside.

Five squid and three blue crabs later, Stella was heading back from the Reefer, her pockets full of change. She was pleased with the morning's entrepreneurial success. When she got back to Marcel, she saw he was not alone and was strangely reluctant to make eye contact. Standing with him was the Chief Administrator, a small but stocky Nipponese.

The official apparatus of the Farm rarely interacted with the kids, but when it did, the chubby Chief Administrator was its sharp pointy end. Both Marcel and Stella had spent a fair share of their evenings painting walls or scraping barnacles, in penance for acts of sabotage against the 'communal wellbeing—or, more seriously, the profitability of the Farm.

The Administrator wasn't wearing his 'not angry but disappointed' face, the one Stella associated with rebukes and punitive mopping. Instead, he seemed pale and shy—no, not shy, rather embarrassed, or even guilty.

She was still a few paces away, when she realised something was wrong.

The Administrator started talking; her stomach went tight, squeezing into knots. Her cheeks and ears began to burn. She felt sick; she didn't hear the words.

People are being nice. Yesterday, Marcel had told Stella she could keep all the money from the fish. Now, Guillermo's wife is tugging on the netting and calling up.

"You up there, Stella girl? You okay? I've got a plate of food for you. You're probably starving. Come on down and eat with us."

Dead. Cheap Drugs.

Hanging from a rope hinge at one end of the horizontal drum, the container's original black lid functions as a door. Stella pushes it open and pokes her head out.

"I'm okay, Maria. I'm not hungry really." Then, without waiting for a response, she ducks back inside and lies down.

"Nonsense. Come on down here and have a bite to eat. You can't spend your days up in that little room crying."

She pretends not to hear.

Brain blood. Fish food.

After a while, Maria gives up, muttering as she waddles away. Stella watches as she cuts through the alley between the Pussycat and the Admin Block, heading back to the mothballed pontoon, where she and Guillermo and a dozen other families have their huts. When the coast is clear, she climbs down to retrieve the plate of beans and onions. She is starving and wolfs down the food. It tastes delicious, but doesn't fill the hollowness. She pulls the blanket over her legs and lets herself drift into a catatonic trance, which slowly turns into sleep.

She spends the following days in the same state, barely leaving the confines of her 'room' and timing her bathroom trips to minimise the chances of meeting other humans.

***

Choppy surf, driven by the squall, skips across the back of the huge waves beating at the Farm; behemoths sliding like glaciers across yesterday's calm. Rain and spray drum on the thick plastic skin of her bin. Ropes creak and the wind wails. It's the first big storm of the season. Stella lets the colossal sound of the wind and seas and the continuous musical vibration of the ropes pass through her body. She hopes the volume and intensity will crowd out emotions and thought.

Suddenly, the lid door is pulled open and a blast of warm wind and salty spray slams inside. She lunges forward to secure the door again, but this time it isn't the wind that has breached her sanctuary. A drenched boy heaves himself inside and lies, panting and grinning, on the curving floor. Stella is so shocked by the dramatic entrance that her first thought isn't to scream and kick him out. She just sits at the far end of the cylinder and watches.

Marcel takes the absence of hostility as an invitation to stay; his smile broadens and he reaches his hand into his coat. He takes out what looks like a pair of goggles with a thick elastic headband. Stella recognises them straight away. The contractors sometimes amuse the kids by letting them look through the lenses at strange worlds, far below the waves.

"You stole some Spex!"

"No! I found some. They're broken. Well, half-broken. They were floating inside the pen; they must have got washed in or something. They're for you."

It's been six months since her mother succumbed to the dirty poison meth. She is now resting in pieces throughout the South Pacific marine food chain. Stella is bored of grieving and exhausted by constantly worrying about the future. She smiles and accepts the glasses. They are light, not much heavier than shades. She looks at Marcel, who nods encouragingly. She puts them on, pushing the elasticated headband, studded with small metallic discs, over her hair to hold the Spex snuggly in place. Initially, the lenses are opaque; then the left one flickers with polygonal fractal static and comes to life.

It's as if the left screen has become transparent. The image of her room is a bit brighter than normal and looks orange. The right lens remains resolutely blank. It gives an annoying flicker of colour every second or so, seemingly at random.

"Yeah, like I said, they are half-broken," said Marcel. "We can tape that one up on the inside, so it doesn't bother you."

After a few seconds, some blinking text superimposes itself over the view, stars appearing, one after another at five-second intervals. She waits impatiently.

```
CALIBRATING ************
*** ERROR — EEG Transducer Failure ***
*** WARNING — No Symbolic Transmission Possible ***

Look at the left blue sphere
Look at the right blue sphere
```

```
Concentrate on the left blue sphere
Concentrate on the right blue sphere
Think yes
Think No
Look at the left red sphere
```

Then, the Spex are talking to her. They sound faint, high-pitched and tinny, until she finds the dangling buds and pushes them into her ears.

"Can you hear this? Think yes or no."

```
*** ERROR—EEG Transducer Failure. Adjust Headband and try
again. ***
```

"Can you hear this? Blink twice for yes."

She follows the tutorials that suggest themselves, once the initial calibration has run its course. She half notices Marcel get up to leave and is aware, on some level, that time is passing. She does not notice that he is smiling. Later, when the rocking becomes severe, she wedges herself against the curving wall with a pillow and blanket.

The storm is picking up outside. The tortured scream of the wind manages to force its way past her ear buds. It howls around the ropes that attach her feed bucket to the struts and girders that support the building. Outside, massive slabs of water are queuing for their turn to slam into the fragile little floating collection of objects. On the other side of the ring, that is bearing the brunt of the storm, cranes are being ripped from the decks; entire buildings vanishing in a breath. Stella is oblivious to it all; she has found something to absorb her mind and to deny it any chance to rage and wail.

The crew of the sewerage barge are lashing more lines to the farm, trying to stop themselves from tearing loose. Every time the sea drops from beneath them, the boat hangs above three metres of empty air. When the storm fills the void again, a hammer of water slams back against their steel hull.

Only yesterday, Marcel's father ran another set of lines around Stella's pod. He looped coils of webbing through the galvanised steel gantries. Stella doesn't really care if she dies; she is busy paging through menus.

A massive set of waves break, one after the other, across the three-hundred-metre hoop, which is the Farm. Stella is on the trailing perimeter, but avalanches of water still periodically douse the entire building. The noise is astonishing, but the ties hold.

She pauses while the maelstrom sucks at her plastic shell, waits until the world sorts itself out, then returns to the maze of menus. She is frustrated with the slow progress and repetitive nature of the tutorials. She wants to connect to something, see something real, beyond the farm, its all too familiar buildings and dull poverty-stricken peasants. She randomly dives into the menus again, their glyphs appearing, as she navigates the labyrinth of possibilities. More nested menus appear in response to her choices. She sees something promising:

```
-> Connect
-> Compatible Local Hosts
-> Closest
-> Link . . .
```

Noise cancellation drops down around her like a shell, enveloping her in an insulated fluffy cave of peace. The sounds outside are all but gone, her vision is limited to whatever her Spex choose to show to her left eye. Stella's consciousness severs its ties with her body. Then, finally, she is looking through the eyes, or at least one eye, of another living creature.

Her point of view is in the water, looking up at the bottom of a damaged boat. It is moored alongside the Farm to one of the huge pontoons. She almost quits in frustration. She is still confined to her hoop world. The POV swims higher, towards the bottom of the boat. There is a large crack in its fibreglass hull about twenty centimetres wide. Its source, a torpedo-shaped buoy, is still wedged in the crack. A nose, now trying to nudge through the crack, brushes the buoy. It jerks sideways and rises deeper into the boat, forcing a mass of bubbles from the fissure. Something dark comes into view, and a human arm drops in slow motion, then sways in the water, at one with the waves. Stella is terrified by the apparition, but so is the dolphin. She knows it's a dolphin, because there is a little two-dimensional stylised icon of a dolphin at the top of her vision, which she can see when she focuses on it.

The dolphin dives deeper at a sprint, and then hangs in the water, looking up at the moving liquid geology of the surface. It lets itself drift warily up again and returns to nudge at the crack and the arm. Stella senses a change and feels the dolphin relax in the water. Simultaneously, words appear on the Spex and through her ears:

"Help him. He is not dead." After a few seconds, another message: "Help him."

Stella doesn't know what to do as she quit the tutorial before it got to sending messages.

"Help him. Help him. Help him. Help him. Help him. Help him. Help him…" the voice nags.

Stella pulls on a waterproof jacket and hat and clambers down the ladder from her eyrie. While immersed in the electronic sensory deprivation of the Spex, she had become used to the dolphin's perspective and is shocked by the terrible weather. She leans into the wind and runs in the direction of the boat she knows must be moored not far away, but is utterly obscured by the driving rain and spray. She runs while avoiding the migrating drift-crap tossed up by the sea and then driven by the wind across the ring. She can see the boat.

Old Tommy Sugar is out in his yellow oilskin, tying tarpaulin against his shop. Stella runs to him and grabs his sleeve. It is almost too loud to talk, but he seems to understand some of what she is screaming over the wind and wave roar. He finishes off a knot and starts after her when she dashes away towards what she hopes is the right boat. It is a broken thing, intermittently dashing against the floating concrete pontoons. It's lashed to one leg of the Farm, the loop of rope caught on the barnacles the only thing stopping it from sinking.

Tommy listens to her explain again, and then, without a word, clambers onto the debris-strewn boat. Stella pulls the Spex back down and is instantly transported back to the amniotic stillness of the sea. Her new friend is still down there, looking up at the allegedly not dead fingers. Tommy has been gone less than a minute when she notices the arm twitch. It disappears back up through the crack. She pulls the Spex away again. Squinting against the salt and wind, she watches for movement. Thirty seconds later, Tommy's head pops out of the little cabin, and he is back, carrying a sodden black shape on his back. He looks over at Stella and nods once, before striding off towards the Medical Centre.

Stella watches the body on his back for signs of life as it is hauled through the blasting chaos of the storm. The wind sucks the air out of her lungs and hurls grit, debris and stinging water at her face. She huddles down, behind a stack of nets, covered in tarpaulin. Here, she is safe from the full force of the wind and looks down at the surging flotsam-speckled briny surface. The flickering of electric lights, smashed by the storm, jams her senses. She already misses the peace and tranquillity of below.

Pulling the Spex down over her eyes, she escapes again to the world beneath the huge surging mirror. She is looking at a fractured reflection of a grey torpedo with a mischievous smile. She rises closer to her reflection until two noses meet. Then, she passes the interface and finds herself looking at a girl crouching in the wind and spray, her coat flapping open, ineffectually tied with a length of blue twine. A fifteen-year-old girl, small for her size, with wild straggly hair and a pair of Spex hiding her eyes.

With a near audible click of perspective, Stella is examining herself. She is surprised to see that she is pretty, despite being tatty and poor. Then she lifts her Spex and scans the waves for her watcher, until she finds a slick bulbous nose and tiny black eyes. The nose jerks back and she hears a faint twittering above the wind's roar. A fraction of a second later, her Spex display the incoming message.

"Hello."

Stella walks to the steps, clutching the rusty railing tightly as the wind tries to tear her hair and clothes from her body. She descends as close to the sea as she dares. It is sheltered from the wind and the full force of the waves here, but the swell is two metres and, when the sea withdraws, it does so with a terrifying sucking power. The nose swims closer. Stella is hypnotised, and something happens inside her soul. She feels its love. Then she is sobbing, crying, raging. The eyes watch and wait as a girl, who has seen too much for her fragile mind to process, flails at the universe. When she eventually exhausts herself, she feels stupid and embarrassed. She smiles shyly at the nose.

"Hello," it repeats.

"Hi," she replies, self-consciously.

```
*** ERROR–EEG Traducer Failure ***
*** WARNING–No local symbolic Transmission Possible ***
```

There is a pause and then more chattering, accompanied by another audible message: "Can you talk?"

She doesn't know much about how the Spex work, but she knows they are broken and so she shakes her head and then blows her nose on her fingers, flicking the snot into the sea. The dolphin doesn't show any signs of understanding, so she shouts as loud as she can:

"Yes, I can talk!"

The increase in volume seems to have done the trick. She guesses the Dolphin also has something like Spex that will translate her voice only if it can hear the words.

"Can you hear me?" the dolphin asks.

Stella nods. Then, still not sure if dolphins understand human body language, she shouts. "Yes. Will you be my friend?"

```
I am Tinkerbell [@Tinkerbell899 Free Dolphin, Pics, Blog,
Personal].
Thank you for helping Chris [@ChrisTuck3rR, Marine Geol-
ogist, Recent Publications, Blog, Personal].
Who are you?
```

"Will you be my friend, Tinkerbell?" she shouts above the raging surf and screaming wind. She needs this so badly; it threatens to tear her in half. The sobbing hysteria is close.

```
I am Tinkerbell [@Tinkerbell899 Free Dolphin, Pics, Blog,
Personal].
```

"Please?" she shouts. "My mother died. I don't have friends… well, except Marcel. He is the boy who gave me these." Her voice dies to a mutter. "But he is… can you even understand me?"

"I understand," the voice says. "Who are you?"

This is followed by some arcane debug messages:

```
*** DIAGNOSTIC - Audio Verbal Translation Error Report:
High levels of background noise 17%. Semantic Incompati-
bilities 40%. ***
```

"I am Stella, Stella Sagong," she shouts. More text appears

across her vision:

[@St3llaSag0ng LOCAL_GUEST, no details added]

Stella doesn't understand half of the weird text displayed by the Spex. However, as far as she is concerned, the next words to appear on the scratched lens are the best message ever sent from one entity to another.

Tinkerbell has added you [@St3llaSag0ng LOCAL_GUEST, no details added] as a friend.

The hand is black. Skin, once supple, now charcoal brittle and split. Cracks showing a pink wetness deep within, weep with clear liquid. Nails shift in the sticky raw flesh or are missing from charred stumps. A hand closes on his neck, the flesh of its palm shifting and disintegrating like the puffy skin of an over-boiled chicken. The grip tightens, sloughing more skin as it twists. He feels the cool of bare gelatinous muscle touching the sensitive skin of his throat. He knows it's a dream, even as he dreams, but the knowledge doesn't help. Reality is worse. A man is dead, and he knows the mangled, burnt, water-saturated body is floating somewhere on the Rheine or is already slowly drifting west, across the sea on its last journey.

Some part of Anosh decided to wake up then. Without turning on the light, he carefully slid out of bed and shuffled across the bedroom to change his sweat-soaked t-shirt. It was 4.30 am. Out of the sanctuary of their bed, the room was icy cold. The sense of horror, spawned by the dream, felt too big and too real to be contained within his skull. It wouldn't let itself be rationalised away by the process of waking. He needed to check that nothing evil had spread out of his eyes and mouth into the real world.

He walked along the carpeted hall into the boys' room and leant over each, carefully listening for the rhythm of their gentle breathing. Satisfied that they were okay, he pulled his dressing gown around himself and, against all instincts, took the dark stairs to the roof. His heart was still hammering, and the dream wouldn't leave him. He sat on one of the wrought iron chairs Ayşe had reclaimed. A half-moon lit snowy roofs and streets, veiled by wisps of cloud, an eye peering out between fingers. Its light illuminated fog rising from the river and smoke from a few chimneys.

Over time, a resentful stand-off with the local gangs had established itself. Many vigilante self-defence forces had sprung up. The police rarely interfered, and this had been taken as a sign. Anosh could see tiny glimmers of red on several of the surrounding roofs, glowing ends of cigarettes, flaring and dimming or disappearing entirely behind the cupped hands of sentinels. In the years since they had moved in, the Docks had developed a reputation for self-sufficiency. They now attracted a steady stream of artists and artisans. The neighbourhood hadn't seen such levels of occupancy since the nineteenth century.

In a form of self-assembly, micro brewers, coders, cabinet makers, modders, tinkers, electricians, mechanics and other like-minded can-do-ers flocked to its run-down warehouses and empty office buildings. The darker side of this auto-ghettoisation was that individuals deemed incompatible were encouraged to move along; cajoled, bullied, and forced out by enthusiastic members of self-appointed local committees.

The cold slowly washed terror from the shadows. Normality returned and eventually he felt secure enough to get back into bed. In his absence, the sweat that had soaked his pillow had turned cold and clammy. He flipped it round before lying down. Reluctantly, he surrendered his mind to the realm of sleep again.

The next day, the terrors were replaced by the mundane routine of family life. A week had passed since the shooting. The first night, ebbing adrenaline had left him exhausted, and he had gone back to sleep immediately. The nightmares did not start until the third night. The imagined horror had wiped out any clear memory of the actual event. He was beginning to think that, somehow, the night had been a communal dream; there was no body, had never been a body.

Their daily routine started with him cleaning out the ashes and lighting a little fire. Ayşe would get up a few minutes later and put the water on to boil for brewing the morning's tea or coffee, depending on what was available. After Anosh had washed his face and checked that nothing was amiss with the house or roof, they would take their mugs to the window and stand looking out at the activity on the street. It was a special time for them; they chatted while waiting for the kitchen to warm up before waking the boys for school. The walls were still bare chipboard. They had hung blankets for doors, and their dwelling was tolerably warm, once the fire was lit. That morning, Ayşe was about to pour their second cup when, from downstairs, the mechanical bell rang with a dull trill.

Anosh's heart immediately began to race. Denial and the fervent hope that their society was too dis-functional to support a functioning police force evaporated as he looked down from the window: a battered silver and white auto was pulled up at the curb and two men in smart green uniforms stood at their door.

The automatic buzzer had never worked, so Anosh went down the stairs to confront the visitors.

"Guten Morgen. Sind Sie Herr Anosh Karum? Durfen wir rein kommen?"

"Er…" Anosh paused, but he couldn't think of any valid reason the two policemen shouldn't enter. "Yes, of course. Come in."

He led the men up the three flights of steps to their kitchen and the four sat facing the stove. Ayşe distributed drinks.

The older of the two visitors seemed in no hurry to get to any point. He was an elderly chap with a big white moustache, ruddy cheeks and a belly that, despite rationing, appeared to be thriving. His position clearly granted him privileged access to bratwurst and beer. He sat cupping his hot tea and smiling pleasantly, while politely letting his eyes drift around the kitchen, sliding from flowers to fruit bowl and settling on their radio.

His colleague was much younger, probably less than twenty-five, hawkish nose, with neat, mousey-blond hair combed diagonally across his forehead. He kept glancing from face to face, looking to his boss for clues on how to proceed.

After a few awkward minutes, Anosh asked: "So, can we help you with anything?" Ayşe flicked her eyes over to him and then down to the floor. Anosh was aware that the old cop was taking all of it in, every glance, word and breath.

"Can you help us? I suppose you could." He paused dramatically, while looking into their souls—years seemed to creep by. "I noticed as we were walking by that, unlike in most areas of this humiliated city, my Companion has a data connection. I also notice that, although there's a scheduled power outage at the moment, your lights are on."

Anosh was thrown off balance, unsure if he was expected to say anything.

The younger cop took out his Companion and was thrilled to find he could access the community OpenMesh gateway. With a bit of tapping and the odd muted exclamation, the tinny, but still familiar, tones of a popular classic soap opera began to emanate from the Companion's little speakers. They were all looking at him. As if stricken, Anosh realised that professional suspect interrogation protocol did not include watching re-runs of old daytime TV. The senior policeman smiled indulgently, but gestured to the younger cop that he should stop playing and pay attention.

"It's nice to see the internet, or the Mesh, as I think it's now called, popping up again. It's such a powerful tool for education and community."

The geek in Anosh wanted to explain that the two things were different, but the old cop continued.

"I don't find it so much of an inconvenience as some of my younger colleagues." He glanced at the aforementioned individual, who continued to look sheepish.

Again, Anosh had the feeling he should say something. Instead, he remembered Vikram's instructions for dealing with the police and took a sip of his tea, staying silent.

They supped and chatted for another half an hour, until Segi wandered in, rubbing his eyes and making for the food cupboard.

The older policeman smiled at the sleepy boy.

"Say good morning, Segi," Ayşe said.

He looked up as if noticing the two strangers for the first time.

"Hi," he said, still sixty per cent asleep. He took a bowl from below the sink and some oats and raisins from a jar. "Do we have any milk?"

"No, just the powder."

"Oh, man!" Segi complained, spooning in some yellowish powder and running hot water from the kettle into the bowl. He stirred the mixture with a spoon, went to a clear bit of work surface and leant on one elbow, while proceeding to shovel the food into his mouth.

"Right, Wolfgang. Enough sitting around and drinking tea!" the old policeman exclaimed, breaking them all out of a spell. The adults had been watching Segi, who was quite oblivious to any tension or atmosphere, as he ate his breakfast.

"Yes, boss."

"Well, very nice of you to stop by," Ayşe said. "If you give me some warning next time, I can bake something for you both."

Anosh was astonished at how relaxed Ayşe was able to be.

"Absolutely. It was a pleasure to meet you and your lovely

family," the cop said sweetly, while taking her hand.

Anosh thought he might even kiss it. Instead, he turned to Anosh.

"Take care of your family, Mr Karum," he said significantly, his voice losing its jovial tone for the first time. "There are a lot of hungry, angry people around these days."

"Yes, of course," Anosh stammered. "Thanks."

Ayşe showed the policemen back down the steps to the door. Once they were gone, Anosh allowed himself to slump into a chair.

"He knew!" he said to Ayşe once she returned.

"Of course he knew! He just wanted to make sure you weren't a psychopath and weren't going to make a habit of shooting people. Now, don't worry; it's all okay," she said, squeezing onto the chair next to him and holding him tightly.

They ate a small breakfast together, and the boys went off to their school around the corner. About thirty local kids attended. It was run by two retired schoolteachers out of what had once been a CoffeeHut. There was some good-humoured speculation whether the two women were spinsters or lesbians. Parents paid what they could afford, usually in barter or MeshCoins, but most of the funds to keep it going came with the kids from the walled estate up the river.

There, corporate employees and other members of the

vestigial official economy still lived in a 1990s parallel universe theme-park. Their left-wing, champagne socialist parents mollified their wealth guilt by sending their kids to a community school. This patronage, more than anything else, was probably responsible for the tolerant attitude of police and local government to all the Dock's squatting and self-sufficiency.

In the afternoon, after lessons, it was time for chores. Anosh was working on the plans for a photo-bioreactor, basically a broad ladder of transparent tubes connected for farming Spirulina and other algae. Ayşe was preparing dinner and would probably spend a significant portion of her afternoon waiting in line to cash in the family's cheese and butter vouchers. Zaki and Segi had been given the job of delivering eggs as a down payment against the bioreactor's crucial Perspex tubes. By complex negotiation Segi, the youngest, ended up with all the walking, while Zaki promised to provide close air support, POVing with their latest quad drone. Anosh had listened absent-mindedly to the discussion, but decided that, at thirteen, Segi was old enough to stand up to his brother's badgering and a walk across town would do him good.

***

Segi slammed the door and set off up the street. A few people were about and some smiled or waved as he passed. After a couple of minutes' walk, he left the Docks community, and people began merely to nod or ignore him entirely. He steeled himself for the trip across hostile territory. Best to look confident, busy and angry, rather than like a defenceless boy out on his own with a bag full of precious eggs.

Getting into the role, he kicked at a bottle lying in his way and sent it careening into a wall, where it smashed into shards. He was startled at the result and quickly looked around, then up towards the faint, high-pitched whine. Nobody seemed to have noticed his wanton vandalism. Nobody was watching. He was walking beside the mostly deserted pot-holed road, which curved around a huge traffic island. The roundabout was chequered with small allotments, and there were several people weeding or watering. He was approaching a run-down street with a multi-storey car park on one side and a derelict garage on the other.

Much of the infrastructure, formerly devoted to automobiles, was unused or abandoned. This part of town had none of the vibrancy of the Docks. Nothing was made or repaired here. This was where the broken pieces of society came to sleep and pass their lives. Some ladies were standing by the dead traffic lights at an intersection. A chunky auto thundered past, drawing their attention, but there was nobody at the wheel, and it had no intention of stopping. After it had gone, they looked over at Segi, possibly evaluating him as a future customer, but he was not interested in their questionable charms, and there was not enough certainty in their world for them to plan their lives far enough out for him to be relevant.

A group of *Penners* shuffled past, pushing carts full of blankets and newspapers. They were busy with something secret; huddling, swearing, and muttering amongst themselves. They ignored him. He turned off the main road. He hated this bit. The underpass was dark and fetid. Thankfully, there was another way and he wouldn't have to walk through it, but even the expectation of proximity to the mouth of Hades had been enough to fill his whole morning with dread. He walked to the intersection where the autobahn was bisected by a ring road. It was dark in the pedestrian tunnel that once provided a shortcut under the big dual carriageway and now provided dry, 'no rent' accommodation. As he walked past, he pulled out a powerful little torch and let it shine into the tunnel.

Filth covered the floor: shit and slime and old cardboard boxes. Huge, bloated worms turned away from the intrusive beams, muttering in their *Penner* speak, "*verpisdich, dreck,*" "*Arschloch.*" Out of the shadows, a bundle of rags staggered towards the light like a filthy moth. Siegfried turned off the torch and backed away. The *Penner* was muttering nasty things and randomly shouting. Segi just stood and watched as it shuffled up the stairs towards him. He was terrified, transfixed. He nearly dropped the eggs his mother placed so sceptically into his charge. He turned and tripped.

The *Penner* was at the steps. Suddenly, a green beam slapped down out of the sky and slashed across the *Penner's* face. It was followed by two small projectiles that fizzed as they flew overhead. One veered off to the left, before exploding mid-air two metres away from Siegfried's head. The other flew straight as a dart and detonated on contact with the reeling *Penner's* chest, issuing an impressive puff of smoke. Siegfried grinned up at the whirring shape that was their tiny hovering quad drone. It dipped him a curtsey. With one last glance at the hopping, coughing *Penner*, Segi started on his way again towards Klaus's Schrot Eck. A faint sting of capsicum pepper followed after him.

The rest of the journey was uneventful; quiet stretches of

dual carriageway, under-populated terraces, micro-farms growing exotic or mundane produce hidden by condensation in long, transparent plastic tubes. Eventually, he got to the old railway yard that was, according to its proprietor, the best source of scrap this side of Akihabara.

He pushed through a gap between the loosely chained gate and the mesh fence, then trudged up to the once grand motorhome where Klaus lived amongst his junk. A massive ridgeback came barrelling towards him, barking furiously, but the murderous dash turned into a playful skid. This was followed by copious licks once Klaus shouted for him to calm down. His master's tone of voice and Siegfried's familiar smell labelled him as Friend.

"Eggs! You hear that Benny? Eggs!" The dog looked at his master as if expecting him to say more. Klaus, coming down the steps, grinned at Siegfried and took one of the eggs out of the bag. He broke it into a pale blue, plastic dog bowl, where it was immediately and happily lapped up. This act seemed to give equal pleasure to all of the assembled mammals.

"So, twenty eggs today, eh? Don't let your daddy forget to keep them coming! It's twenty each for these little beauties." Klaus pulled back a sheet of tarpaulin and revealed a cluster of Perspex pipes, filmed with green mould, standing against the side of his caravan. "I stripped these from a factory; don't know what they carried, so tell your daddy to give them a good wash!"

"Dad said he'll pay you a hundred for the lot, but you need to drop me and the pipes back today, or it's no deal."

"Sent you to negotiate, did he?"

"No. He just said to tell you that."

There was an uncomfortable pause, which Benny sensed, his tail motionless as he looked eagerly between the two humans. Finally, Klaus chuckled and reached out to ruffle Siegfried's hair with his grubby, oily hand. Benny barked and joined in, jumping up at the boy and licking at his face.

"Okay, okay. You bloody tinkers drive a hard bargain!" Klaus grumbled.

While he was inside grabbing his things, Siegfried attempted to wipe the dog spit and engine grease from his face. They carefully loaded the pipes into the old methane-powered manual drive Toyota, and Siegfried plucked the hovering drone out of the air. The whine died and he climbed into the cab with it on his lap.

"To save the battery," he explained. Klaus looked sceptically at the black chunky drone, with its projecting rotors, and set off to Siegfried's house, with only the minimum of suspicious muttering.

When they got there, his parents were at the kitchen table, talking and drinking tea. Klaus joined them after what seemed to Siegfried to be excessive handshaking. His mum thanked him for delivering the eggs and, finally dismissed, he dashed off to the room he shared with Zaki.

"Let me have a go!"

"I blasted him! At least say thank you!" Zaki chided, but

he was grinning. The copter had been their project for the past six months. Building and programming it had mostly been Zaki's work, but they had scavenged the parts together and pooled their income to buy any bits they couldn't find or borrow. Today was the first time it had seen action.

"Did you see the rockets? They were awesome!"

"One nearly blew my ear off!"

"Yeah, we need to work on them… but that was so cool!"

"Let me have a go!" Siegfried asked again.

"Go on then, but be careful!"

Siegfried took the two offered Companions and checked out the telemetry. One tablet showed the location of the copter on a satellite picture. He put it down on the bed and sat with his legs crossed in front of it. The map updated itself with video from the drone's cameras superimposed over the satellite texture. The other showed video facing forward and a bunch of menus. He held this one like a steering wheel and used it to pilot the drone, still outside resting on the roof of Klaus's truck. Segi commanded it to hover. Zaki stood by nervously, ready to snatch control if anything looked critical. Siegfried smoothly swooped it up, round the side of the building, until it was bobbing just outside their window. He shot the laser through the window onto the wall. The boys looked at it and laughed.

"That's just dazzle mode," said Zaki. "I'm gonna change it, so on full power, it will make paper smoke."

"Cool!"

"You better let me bring it back. It's nearly out of power."

"I can do it!"

"No, give it back. It's really difficult to fly in through the window."

"Okay, but can I fly it next time?"

"All right."

Siegfried gave the Companion back to Zaki and pushed open the window. His brother expertly piloted the little vehicle into their room, where it buzzed at shoulder height then dropped gently to the floor, rotors quickly spinning down. The boys swarmed like old-style formula one mechanics around their car.

***

A week later, it was Zaki's turn to deliver the eggs. He carefully wrapped them in towels and placed the bundle into his rucksack. Segi was riding shotgun, remotely piloting the nasty-looking black drone. Ayşe also gave Zaki a bunch of bay leaves and two slices of thick, cheesy potato omelette for Klaus. He dropped these in on top. He had come straight home from school and was about to disappear into his room to get on with some crucial hacking, when Ayşe ambushed him and reminded him of his promise.

He set off at a jog, glancing up occasionally to see how Segi was piloting the drone. He got to the underpass and, conscious of the time he was losing to the stupid chores, took the shortcut under the road, through the dark tunnel. He remembered it from years ago, when they had parked at the big mall complex and came back this way towards the trendy Docks. It was tiled with murals of rivers and animals. Segi even had an octopus on the wall somewhere. He had sent it in for a competition and had won the under-fives or something.

The lamps were out, but it was still light enough to see. Zaki decided to risk it. He trotted down the steps and ran along the tunnel. The mural was still visible in places, but much of it was covered in black grime or smeared with shitty handprints. It stank of piss. The floor was thick with cardboard boxes and plastic bags, full of shit and miscellaneous filth. Zaki quickly regretted the decision, but was already deep into the tunnel and, behind him, worm-like creatures were rearing up and growing arms and heads as the *Penners* clambered out of their sleeping bags. He was two-thirds of the way through, but the commotion of his running feet and the shouts of the disturbed human ghouls behind him were rousing the whole tunnel into a seething, swearing confusion. An arm grabbed him by the sleeve, but he pulled away. Far behind him, he heard the amplified buzz as Segi took the drone into the tunnel.

Damn! Segi should have taken the other way to come down from the front. A bunch of *Penners* were forming a wall in front of him at the bottom of the steps. If he could get past them, he could probably make it. He unslung the rucksack and reached in to take out an egg.

"Eier?" he said, softly lobbing the egg underarm to one of the *Penners*, who instinctively caught it and looked at the clean, white object in his hands.

Zaki stopped running and took another couple of eggs out the pack and placed them carefully on the ground to one side of the passage. The *Penners* exchanged looks and then shoved each other as they fought for the prospect of the delicious protein. Zaki dashed the other way, though they were barely paying him any attention anymore. He loped up the steps two at a time and into the fading evening light.

A couple of minutes later, Segi eventually piloted the little drone out of the tunnel. At first, he couldn't see his brother and was about to head off at full speed towards Klaus's. Then, as he rotated his POV, he noticed a bundle of clothes lying at the curb. As he flew closer, it resolved into the crumpled form of a boy. The rucksack was gone from its back. Blood was on the tarmac, smeared as if the whole body had been dragged through it by the one hand that was still outstretched; its fingers clenched on nothing.

Zaki had barrelled out of the tunnel, straight into a gang of older kids playing some game with a deflated ball. They had pushed him. He had stumbled onto his ass, and they had laughed.

They demanded the contents of his bag, but stopped laughing when he told them to "fuck off".

He tried to get to his feet, but they beat him down. Then they kicked him. When they could not pry the strap of the bag from his fingers, they kicked him some more. He coughed and sobbed as the kicks landed, smashing into his ribs and face.

It went quiet and he slipped into blackness; but awakened immediately, screaming. One of the boys had grabbed his arm and, after deliberately placing it on the curb, had stamped down, shattering the bones.

A final round of massive kicks to his ribs and they had tugged the bag from his limp fingers and run off.

The drone was too late. Now, it hovered over the bleeding body.

Shapes were shuffling out of the dark towards the commotion.

When he lifted the heel of his shoe, there was a sucking click as it pulled clear of the ancient carpet's black, tarry surface. In a small patch by the wall across from their table, the pattern was still fresh: red and maroon with curling fronds of green. It had been covered for thirty years by a fruit machine, which now, incompatible with the modern world, stood outside on the pavement in the rain.

"You haven't said a lot, Keith," Deb remarked. "What's your grand plan?"

Keith looked over to her with heavy eyes; he already had the beginnings of a headache. They had been drinking since four in the afternoon, but obviously he had not been drinking fast enough to keep the metabolic penance at bay.

"Still trying to work that one out. I do have an exciting plan for the next fifteen minutes. Want to hear it?"

She smiled, but shook her head and curled her lip. "Nah, been there; done that!"

"Keith is joining the Old Man's firm, aren't you bud?" Ben chipped in.

"Yes, thought I'd give selling my soul a try."

"Didn't you two go to school together?" the other girl asked. Keith couldn't remember her name. She had arrived with Ben, who claimed he picked her up the night before, but Keith suspected that was a lie, especially as she knew their backstory. Ben probably would not have given her the edited highlights of his life as part of his pre-coital patter. It was more reasonable to assume she was a hostess, paid to smile and be friendly, primed with nuggets of narrative in order to create the illusion that there were human beings who didn't find Ben repugnant. Keith didn't really give a shit either way.

"Yeah, and what a thrill that was!" Keith said. "I was one of the token poor people they let in to keep the lynch mobs off their backs."

"It's true," said Ben, "he always was a tight wad!"

"Hey! I just got the drinks. Go and uncurl some of your crisp new notes and buy us a round!"

Ben took one out of his pocket, crumpled it up, and chucked it at Shaun. "Be a darling, Shaun. I'm all squashed in here with Melanie."

Shaun picked up the note, without comment, to make a run to the bar. The poor little tosser had been Ben's gofer since seventh grade.

Melanie, so that was her name. He looked at Ben, slobbering all over the fragile girl. She was rather attractive. He supposed she might not be a hostess. There was the possibility she was just some poor company employee, who miscalculated in thinking an evening getting her face covered in Ben's saliva would be a fair trade for some future promotion or perk.

Deb leant towards Keith, looking significantly over at Ben. "Why are you doing this?"

"What?"

"Going to work for little Lord Ass-hole over there?"

"Oh, don't fucking start."

"Seriously, you hate all that shit! They are tight with the *Forwards* you know. 'Government-sponsored secret police', you used to call them."

"Yeah, well, I'm not thrilled either. It's okay for you; you're an artist. You've got your life sorted."

She looked at him incredulously. "I live in a squat on handouts from a system I despise. Get real. I am only drinking with this twat because he promised to buy a couple of rounds, and I can't afford both paint and beer at the moment."

"But at least you know what you want!" said Keith. "I don't have a clue, and I guess, when it comes down to it, I would rather get paid well doing basically anything, than waste my fucking life in pointless poverty!"

"That's the opposite of what you said last time, darling, during your last existential crisis of being."

"I know." He took another gulp of beer and tried to go back to studying the carpet.

"You still owe me for talking you out of joining the army! Oh well, at least you will be able to buy me dinner every now and again. I might even consider getting back together with you."

The carpet lost some of its interest. "Sleeping with the enemy doesn't sound like your thing."

Deb leant over to slap him gently on the cheek. "Who knows, Keith dear. You're not the only one with flexible morals. Spoil me and we'll see."

"Ha!" Ben chortled. "You see, Keith. The perks of wealth and power!"

Keith hadn't realised Ben was listening. He turned to reply, taking in Ben's grinning, self-satisfied mug and Melanie's lightly masked look of horror and self-disgust. They made eye contact for a second, then she shrugged and looked away. Shaun returned with a round of drinks, complete with Jäger chasers.

Ben slapped him on the shoulder. "Nice one, Shaun! Good call with the Jäger!"

Ironically, Keith realised Ben was the least hypocritical person at the table. He was buying friendship and was comfortable with that. No moral torment for him. Keith decided he would try to pause the destructive introspection by getting very, very drunk. He raised his little glass of brown, syrupy liquid to Melanie and winked. She hesitated for a second and then returned the gesture. It looked like she had come to a similar decision. He shuffled along the bench towards her slightly, and they clinked glasses. Ben read the moment expertly and slid over to the chair next to Deb; he knocked the tray, which tipped over her shot. Without a word, he reached out and took the glass from in front of Shaun and passed it to Deb. She looked over to Keith and Melanie, now laughing conspiratorially at some private joke. Then she sighed and took the proffered glass.

The next day, Melanie had left early with little conversation. She was presumably horrified to be waking up in Keith's tiny, dingy flat, rather than one of Ben's penthouse apartments. Keith cleaned his teeth, took two Feel-Betters, showered, and got dressed. He set off across London to meet Ben for the drive up to Aberdeen. The cold cleared his head, and the tube ride allowed a few minutes of recuperation. As he got out at High Street Kensington, he was eyed suspiciously by police or security officers—it was difficult to tell which, without reading the fine print on their badges.

Let in by an obsequious housekeeper, Keith sat across the ancient polished oval table from Ben and his father. They both wore suits of deep, rich material; fine pinstripes, in Ben's case, and navy blue for the father. Keith was wearing his only suit, a thin polyester affair that looked like a disposable paper jumpsuit in comparison.

Ben's leather luggage was stacked neatly by the front door. Keith's tatty wheelie stood next to it. Ben had offered to drive him up to the office in Aberdeen in his two-seater. The alternative was to risk the crumbling public transport infrastructure. It was a choice of sitting next to a babbling piss-soaked tramp on a plastic seat or sunk into a glove of heated leather next to Ben. It had been a close thing, but here he was. Aberdeen would be Keith's home office for the first six months, and Ben had business up there, or had created some.

They drank some spectacularly nice coffee out of paper-thin

porcelain cups, poured from a pot that looked like it had been cut from a solid chunk of metal.

Ben noticed Keith looking at the coffee pot. "We had this carved from a big block. It's two kilos of solid platinum, worth a fortune."

"Doesn't all that cold metal make the coffee go cold too quickly?"

"Yes, it's a silly affectation. But it makes a point. Sometimes, it's the point that is important," Ben's father said, not taking his eyes away from his printed paper.

To Keith, they had never looked more alike, or more like sharks; pudgy sharks with hook noses, big floppy ears, and bushy eyebrows.

"Anyway, we just have the maid warm it up, no big deal," Ben said.

"Better set off, Ben, if you want to get a night's sleep before tomorrow," Ben's father said.

"Sure thing, Paps. Ready Keith?"

"Yes, thanks for the coffee and the Danish."

"Glad you're joining us, Keith. There's lots of work to do, and lots of opportunity for a bright young man in my company." George Baphmet stood and extended his hand. Keith pushed back his chair and shook the extended appendage.

"Thanks for the opportunity. I hope I won't disappoint you."

They took a lift down into the basement of the huge Georgian town house and piled the suitcases into the back of the sleek British Racing Green two-seater. A massive garage door slid open, disappearing into the wall, and Ben gunned the engine, sending a deafening roar echoing off the low ceiling and gloss-painted walls. They tore out onto mostly empty streets and across the city, heading for the M6 and the North.

The landscape was a grey smear—smoke, fog, and naked concrete, drawing stripes across the brown and puce of the northeast winter. They were five hours out from London and still had three to go. Ben had shut up for a few minutes, and Keith was making the most of it, letting his eyes jump from feature to feature like a sprinting acrobat as the car ate up the miles. The FastLane™ was virtually empty, but plenty of decrepit vehicles were chugging along the broken tarmac of the public lanes next to them.

Two tier roads; two tier schools; Morlocks and Eloi.

They passed clusters of parked buses and lorries, knotted with lines and webs of tarpaulin. Dirty kids and dogs played in the mud. More often than he expected, they passed the formally arranged, but equally bleak, government camps. The fences, razor wire, and dazzling LED arrays distinguishing them from their ad hoc equivalents.

Eventually, Ben's machine glided to a halt in front of the granite edifice that was Aberdeen's Foster Hotel. Ben had reserved a suite for them for the night. Tomorrow, Keith would join the induction event and be ingested by BHJ.

A youth in a silly hat picked up Ben's suitcase, but left Keith to tug his scruffy wheelie from the vestigial back seat of Ben's car and lug it into the reception on his own. They got up to their room, and Ben pressed a fifty into the boy's hand.

Ben chose one of the adjoining rooms and flopped down onto its bed.

"Grab me a beer from the fridge, would you?" he shouted.

"Get it yourself, you lazy arse!"

"Shit! I drive you up here, splash out on the best hotel in the city and I'm going to take you on the biggest shag-fest piss-up since the Coronation, and you won't pass me a beer!"

"Christ! There you go," Keith said fetching the bottle from the little mahogany fridge. "So what are we going to do tonight, then?" he asked, his curiosity piqued.

"Don't know," Ben admitted shrugging. "But I've got my BHJ corporate card and my best buddy by my side."

Again, Keith couldn't be sure if Ben genuinely didn't know what a friend was and thought the label could be correctly applied to their relationship, or if it was just more from the babbling brook of sales patter that poured eternally from Ben's lips, like some mythical Fountain of Bullshit.

They left the hotel in a taxi that took them to what passed for a trendy nightclub in depression era Aberdeen. The door was controlled by two fearsome-looking blokes, strapped with both lethal and less than lethal side arms and every sort of tactical gadget possible. One was simply colossal and intimidating in the way of a bull or gorilla. The other was small, wiry, and red-haired, drawing his own power to unsettle from his aura of barely controlled, psychopathic fury. Keith shuffled past them, looking at the floor, and was horrified when he looked back to see Ben striking up a conversation with the two. He was determined not to let Ben drag him into another of the 'situations' that arose, apparently spontaneously, in his immediate vicinity.

At school, Keith had often been slapped in the face by the vortex of shit that Ben Baphmet left in his wake. He chose to ignore the conversation and cleared the area without delay, heading straight to the bar instead. He was joined a few minutes later by Ben, who was now grinning ear to ear, having somehow befriended the scary thugs and scored a gram of Charlie. Keith shook his head and accepted the two pints from the barman, who was eyeing the plastic Ziploc bag, and the white powder inside, suspiciously. Ben insisted on paying and excessively tipping the barman, who quickly became a tower of beaming smiles.

The car, the hotel room, bouncers who dispensed bags of coke instead of beatings: Keith was constantly reminded why he hated Ben, but he took the bag to the gents, and the evening took a wild lurch for the better. When Keith woke at 10.30 am the next day, with the worst hangover of his life and already half an hour late for his induction, he had to admit Ben had been good to his word; it had been a monstrous night.

A text from Melanie was waiting on his Companion. Money, power, and female companionship—Welcome to the Dark Side.

Traffic was working its way around a massive gouge in the road. A water main had ruptured—months ago—and the torrent had been patiently eroding the road ever since. Their driver was reading from a Companion on his lap, not paying attention as the limo nudged forward every time a small gap opened up between them and the car in front. Ben watched a group of kids filling buckets and then balancing them on the crossbars, or hanging them off the handlebars of big, beaten-up, old racing bikes. A woman was crouched down, washing clothes in a big plastic baby bath. He knew he should be used to it by now, but was still shocked to see such a Third World scene painted with the urban UK grimy colour palette.

Finally, they bumped up onto the pavement and cleared the bottleneck. The driver took the wheel for a minute when the vehicle balked at driving onto a pedestrian designated area. Eventually, they made it back onto roads free of gridlock and natural disasters and arrived a few minutes late at the Ministry of Sport and Entertainment.

Apart from a single broken ground floor window, covered in a huge sheet of weathered plywood, the building looked well-maintained. Here, at least, there was the illusion of a functioning civic structure.

Ben's father climbed out, brushing his suit straight and gathering his dainty Italian leather briefcases. The doorman barely looked at their IDs, paying much more attention to the prominent labels on their kit and clothes; justifiably so, brand logos were always harder to counterfeit than government IDs. They paid the courtesy of going through the security scan, even though it was not working, then received their patting down. Ben barely flinched as a gloved hand cupped his testicles and then wriggled along the crease of his arse. He was wearing a nice new pair of Spex, which were cool enough to pique the interest of even this jaded security goon. Under some frail pretext, these were demanded and poured over. Ben could barely restrain from shouting and snatching them back as he watched the buffoon put his greasy fingerprints all over the lenses.

Once they had been suitably humiliated, they were allowed to leave the squalor of the twenty-first century and take the steel and glass elevator up to the fantasyland the new Forward government and their media partners had begun to spin around themselves. Here, webs of half-truths were woven together to convince an increasingly sceptical public that things were not as bad as they seemed. The cocoon took prodigious efforts to maintain and BHJ was hoping to win contracts with their new tech for automating the production of exquisite opinion-influencing lies.

The receptionist, who met them at the elevator, wore a floral dress and flat shoes. She was beautiful—but, more importantly, she was clean and fresh. She held out her hand and smiled. Ben and his father were enveloped in a mist of lavender and bergamot.

"A pleasure to finally meet you, Mr Baphmet."

They followed her past open doors, where groups of whole-some, ethnically diverse, sexually inclusive *experts* strove to elevate the unsanitary hordes with culture, art, and the spirit of competition. Ben smirked and winked at his father to let him know he was in on the sham. Probably nothing these bright-eyed hopefuls would ever write would make it into policy, prose, or pop culture. They were unpaid interns, recruited solely for their Hitler Youth enthusiasm. If they came through again six months later, Ben expected to see the same vegan moccasins and cashmere shawls, but none of the same faces.

"Doctor Pritchard, an honour to meet you, Minister. Thank you so much for finding the time to see us." Ben's father pumped the offered hand and introduced his son as his assistant and protégé.

"The pleasure is mine, Mr Baphmet. Come into my office."

"Please call me George."

"Perfect. Can I offer you both a drink?" Pritchard asked.

This was a tricky one. 'Coffee' would be the standard response, but it would be critically embarrassing for the Minister if the unpredictable ebb and flow of import goods left him temporarily unable to oblige.

"Coffee please," Ben replied instantly, to his father's horror.

Oh well, the damage was done now. "Yes, for me too please."

The Minister nodded to the receptionist hovering in the doorway. She slipped away. The Minister ignored his luxurious leather chair and enormous desk and deigned to join them at the conference table, another elegant piece of furniture that sat next to the glass interior wall of his tennis court-sized office.

"Did you have any trouble finding us?"

"No, not at all," said George. "There was a little engineering work on Upper Brook Street that slowed us down a bit, that's all."

Ben had to choke down a splutter of laughter when he realised his father was talking about the Grand Canyon that had swallowed three lanes and half a building.

"Ah yes, I do hope they find the time to fix that soon," replied the Minister. "It is a nuisance. You have no idea how the people talk, despite all the good work we do here. A little hole in the ground and a few waggling tongues spoils it all."

"How about a nice summer vignette of bare-chested kids splashing in a little water? Who could object to that?" Ben threw in, recovering from his spasm of inappropriate mirth.

"I see your son is not going to have a problem filling his father's shoes!" said the Minister. "Fantastic, let's do it." They all chuckled.

Ben sat and watched the two older men talking. He couldn't work out if the Minister believed all the double speak. It was the thing Keith kept bringing up. Was it all a grand conspiracy, with disciplined actors taking their scripted positions? He didn't know, even now, sitting across from a guaranteed player next to his billionaire father. He didn't know the answer. Perhaps, one day, his father would let him in on the secret—if there was one.

The coffee arrived; it was of the instant variety, thin and bitter.

"Until the WTO can stop the sham economies dumping their counterfeit merchandise on us, we are going to have to live with increased levels of unemployment," said the Minister. "We simply cannot let our constituents lose hope, while they are waiting to get back to work. We have to give them something to cling to."

"Exactly, Minister," Ben's father said. A slight shift in posture and tone indicated they were now moving past pleasantries and onto the meat of the meeting. "That's why we have come today. We would like to show you some new technology that may be able to improve your situation. Ben?"

"Sure, of course," replied Ben. "At BHJ, we have recently pulled back the curtain on what we think may become one of our most important products. We call it the Sage…"

"Like the herb?" Pritchard asked.

"No," replied George. "It's a marketing term, some sort of vague acronym of Synthetic General Intelligence. Silly really, not my idea, but I imagine our marketing department wants our customers to think of wise old men with beards." He gave a wink.

Ben thanked his father with a nod and continued. "Imagine automated, integrated PR. All statements and opinion backed by reams of research. Supported and re-enforced by well-placed sound bites and scripted statements from both real and constructed personalities. Strategic modelling of populations, incorporating adjustments and optimisation, based upon real time feedback from a significant sample of, um…" Ben hesitated, choosing the right word carefully.

"Citizens?" the Minister offered.

"Yes, of course. Ben, I thought you were going to say voters," George quipped wryly. It didn't hurt at this stage to make it clear that they were fully aware of the significance of what was being offered. "How about a demonstration? Ben, if you wouldn't mind?"

Ben had arranged a Companion on the desk, pairing it with the room's AV system, and projected a sample 'This is Life' episode onto the only wall of the office that wasn't a glass window.

Ben went into his rehearsed patter. "What we have here is twenty hours of tie-in content per week. Characters chosen from racially adjusted archetypes and interactions engineered to exploit any talking points you provide, although semantic analysis of the top stories from the public domain will be chosen as default, incorporating mood-defining themes."

They watched the crude, garish cartoon for perhaps thirty seconds, and then the Minister interrupted. "Sorry to be blunt, but it looks like something my kids would have watched… some trash like South Paw or whatever it was called."

Ben paused the video. "No need to apologise. How old are your children, Dr Pritchard?"

"Oh… wait, err, Julie is thirty-four and Adam is… he must be thirty-seven."

"Our core demographic for this channel! Of course, we can make it look much better, photorealistic even with virtual actors, but have you heard of the Uncanny Valley?"

The Minister seemed about to say something then shook his head.

Ben continued. "People find the 'nearly but not quite' to be a lot less pleasing than obvious parody. That's why we choose the comic, cartoon theme. Plus, the thirty to forty-year-olds are familiar with the style from the thousands of hours of content they watched growing up."

"Sorry if I am slow," said Pritchard. "I have read your brochure and am trying to understand… Your computers come up with twenty hours a week of programming, which you say we can control with a team of virtual spin doctors…?"

"Would you like to meet them?" Ben interrupted.

"Ah, now you see, I thought I had understood. How can I meet them if they are not real?" Pritchard asked, clearly losing track.

Ben offered the Minister a pair of wraparound BHJ branded Spex. Pritchard looked sceptically at the technology before accepting them, with a level of disdain that would have been more appropriate if he was being offered a severed finger freshly pulled from a prison shower's plughole. When he finally deigned to place them on his face, they remained in place for the briefest moment before a flash of shock registered, and he quickly ripped them off again. He cast his eyes in a panicked glance over the again empty chairs around the meeting table. Ben smiled as the old man placed the Spex gingerly onto his nose once more.

"Amazing, I have never seen anything as real as this," he said, his voice full of wonder.

For Ben, the table was already crowded with the Sage avatars, generated by BHJ's automated propaganda server. Where empty chairs were available, the software used images superimposed over the real physical objects with accurate topological juxtapositioning of limbs. As there were more spin doctors than stools, the remaining avatars sat on their own virtual chairs.

The virtual people looked very much like the flesh and blood cluttering the Minister's real offices along the corridors; inclusive, young, beautiful, and conservative.

"Sally, tell Dr Pritchard about yourself."

A tall, severe, blonde-haired lady in a loose-fitting grey business suit began to talk. Her voice had a home counties feel to it, but the accent was strange and the rhythm slightly off.

"I am Sally Strong. I have worked for ten years as a writer for BHJ. I am now senior content supervisor for civil order and social outrage."

"Ask her what she thinks of the hole in the road, Minister."

"Err… Hello, Sally. Nice to meet you. Did you notice any

traffic problems on the way here today?"

"Dr Pritchard," replied Sally, "I do not know how you can remain so calm knowing there are vandals and saboteurs about, who are ruining the commutes of half this city. They are walking free, while thousands of hard-working citizens are effectively jailed every morning within their own vehicles, as they sit for hours in traffic. We need to take the bull by its horns and tackle this problem! We need more police, and they need the powers necessary to enable them to deal with these terrorists effectively!"

Ben interjected. "Sally, scene sketch please: Reprobate, drug using teen as protagonist. Vandalism of transport infrastructure. MOT: life-lesson and repentance."

"Sorry... MOT?" the Minister asked.

"Moral of Tale," the Sally avatar replied before Ben or his father could answer.

She caused the projected scene to change: a fat mother in a run-down kitchen whining to her daughter about something was replaced by a street gang of Asian and black kids throwing stones at traffic lights. The movie that played was a rapid, crudely animated storyboard. At the bottom, an elapsed time readout counted towards twenty minutes, about ten times as fast as the finished episode would. A car, unable to see a vandalised red light, ran across an inter-section and smashed into a lady pushing a pram. The baby was thrown out of its crib and was caught by a construction worker, who was in its line of fire. The woman died later in hospital. The baby was adopted by the construction worker, who also found the wayward stone-throwing Asian kid a job and gave him a second chance.

Ben drank his coffee and watched, reluctantly ingesting both forms of evil artificial spew. The Minister was riveted, and when the little epic finished, he actually clapped.

"Fantastic! Really, you hit the nail on the head there, Sally!"

"Thank you, Minister."

Pritchard, still not quite understanding, made small talk with the avatars for a few minutes. Then he took off the Spex and somewhat reluctantly handed them to Ben's father.

"No no! Keep them, Minister. Try them and keep Sally for a few days, too. Even if you eventually decide our services are not right for the Forward Party, we'll be happy to make an admin Sage available to you."

Ben and his father exchanged a fleeting glance.

Most people considered Spex to be just an enhanced display technology. They could create a movie screen from a blank wall or superimpose objects, or even people, over reality. With elegant programming and understanding of the geometry in your local area, Spex could populate your environment with real avatars of people, either physically remote or fully artificial.

Society had incorporated them into day-to-day life as a new iteration of an old technology—treating Spex as fancy TV sets which were worn on the face—without ever spending the time to inspect the implications.

Newer models, like the fancy ones generously presented to the Minister, were not only for output; they were crammed full of sensors, recording everything from ambient sound to the complex electrical and magnetic fields that crawled across the scalp. EEG and MEG sensors embedded in the frames isolated firing patterns from neurons deep within the brain. Exotic mathematical functions identified active regions and cleaned up cortical firing to the point that speech, or motor control, could be pulled from the neural background noise and used in conversational interfaces to command the Spex.

Spex commands were usually sub-vocalised rather than spoken. Familiar with talking to their HomeHub or TV, people gave little thought to how words were heard and understood by Spex. Manufacturers made no big deal of the technology employed. They were happy to let people misunderstand sub-vocalisation as extreme whispering and let them assume super-sensitive embedded microphones were picking up faint sounds, rather than draw attention to their ceaseless brain scanning.

BHJ's white hat security geeks had warned that, if compromised by malicious actors, the ability to control the images presented to a brain, while simultaneously monitoring its subconscious responses, would give unprecedented access to conscious and subconscious mental content. In one scenario, they outlined how a hacker could locate a region of the victim's brain that was active when thinking about their bank account. If this region also became active while the victim looked at a phone number that contained parts of the account's PIN, the hacker could guess at the complete number. To refine the results, these partial guesses could be modified and presented back to the victim to check for a stronger or weaker response. Over time, massive amounts of information could be mined, without the subject ever guessing they were being interrogated.

The management at BHJ had listened to the security briefing and agreed; this was a shockingly powerful technology that must not be allowed to fall into the wrong hands.

They had, therefore, immediately created a department with sufficient R&D funding to ensure it fell into the right hands.

***

In the 'Card Game' version of human evolution, the assumption has always been that the best an oppressive king can achieve is to postpone the reckoning. A robust hand of sages is a prerequisite for an intelligent, creative society, and necessary for the dynasty's long-term survival. Oppression alienates creativity; drives out the artists. Looking back at their history, the dissidents know it is only a matter of time before base reality re-asserts. Corrupt regimes must crumble to be replaced by open meritocracies—presumably replete with flamboyances of pixies and unicorns.

Lately, this idealistic philosophy has acquired two new problems.

If the entire world is trapped under the same absolute dome of suppression, then there is nobody to out-compete the evil, inefficient rulers and come to the rescue.

Second, one day soon, technology will be ready to replace the troublesome sages and artists with pliant simulacrums; artificial creative power improving the tools of oppression, while keeping the population sedated with an unending stream of synthetic twenty-four-hour media pacification.

Anosh had been sitting at the kitchen table, tinkering with a complicated set of pipes and valves. He heard the appalling scream from beyond the closed doors of Segi's room. Before he had time to react properly, the door slammed open and Segi exploded out. Anosh barely grabbed him as he dashed towards the stairs. It wasn't possible to get any sense out of the boy, other than the words 'Zaki' and 'dead'.

Anosh felt his blood turn cold, but he made the boy put on some shoes, then grabbed the shotgun and dashed out of the house, following his son's frenzied dash.

Anosh's heart was hammering, fingers white as they gripped the black metal. His limbs demanded oxygen, but he had to consciously make an effort to breathe. They sprinted past neighbours.

"Hey, Anosh! What's wrong? Do you need help?" shouted Bernd, a welder and metalworker, who was hitching a trailer to his quad bike.

"Get Vikram!" Anosh called back over his shoulder.

Other pedestrians stopped in their tracks, shocked by the tableaux of an eleven-year-old boy pursued by a bearded man clutching a shotgun. Anosh internally acknowledged this must look disturbing, but he ignored them all, hoping that fear of the gun would prevent anybody interfering.

After five minutes of pavement pounding, he realised where they were heading. The black mouth of the underpass was already yawning open ahead. He put on some speed and passed his son.

"No, Dad, on the other side. Go around!" Segi panted.

Anosh had already been forming a picture of the boy surrounded by a circle of lurking *Penners* in the darkness. He changed direction. Instead of plunging into the tunnel, he vaulted over the railings at the side of the road and ran across the duel carriageway. The underpass was a shortcut below a huge loop of road. A hump, which had once been a manicured and lightly wooded traffic island, was now covered in small fenced allotments. There were angry shouts from a couple of the micro farmers. This was contested territory and persistently plagued by diverse classes of two-legged thieves. The farmers would be armed and not above discharging weapons to protect their precious crops.

Anosh ignored the danger, and everything else around him, crashing through beds of vegetables and trashing the delicate fences that separated the smallholdings. He caught his foot on a wire and fell at full speed into a bamboo trellis, tangling himself up in a mess of raspberry canes and garden wire. When he managed to get up, Segi was only a dozen metres behind. He set off again, leaving the gardens and crossing the opposite circumference of the road. By the time he reached the final barrier, he could already see a small huddle of brown coats. He had twisted his ankle when he fell during the dash and climbed, rather than vaulted, the last metal pedestrian barrier.

Heads were turning as he approached. A few crouching figures stood and stepped away. He chambered a round, sending ahead the distinctive clicking sound as a warning. Eyes followed him from beneath tatty woollen hats. Anosh could see blood on the road. As he limped the last couple of metres, all the *Penners* stood back, leaving a single seated figure cradling the head of a broken doll. The drone was still hovering, letting out its keening whine from a few metres up.

They had carefully picked the limp boy out of the gutter. Anosh carried him to the trailer of the quad bike and cradled his head, while arranging his limp limbs. Vikram and a couple of other neighbours, including Bernd, the owner of the improvised ambulance, were milling around. The *Penners* kept a distance, though they seemed entirely innocent. He learnt that one had covered the boy in a coat and pressed rags to his head to stop the bleeding. Anosh would worry about hepatitis or HIV if Zaki ever woke up. The boy was unconscious, but breathing evenly. Vikram had checked him out, arriving pillion on the quad bike only a couple of minutes after Anosh and Siegfried had turned up.

The 200cc engine barked to life, and they headed back to the Docks. Segi walked back in silence with a few other locals, while Bernd, Vikram and Anosh took the quad.

It was chilly and raining. A group of people were waiting when they got back to the building. They were standing outside the door or on the stairs. They seemed uncomfortably impotent, but ready to help. Ayşe rushed out to grab the child in her arms.

"Careful! We don't know if anything is broken," Anosh warned.

They were trying to move him with minimum disturbance. Ayşe took a floppy hand and squeezed it tenderly. The boy stirred.

"Mama?" Zaki asked weakly. His eyes opened slowly and he took in the cluster of intent faces surrounding him. "What…" he started, turning his head slightly, then wincing in palpable agony. "Mama, my head hurts!"

They took him carefully up to his room and made him as comfortable as they could, while they tried to work out a plan of action. The arm was broken. Vikram guessed he also had a fractured skull, fractured pelvis, and broken ribs. They called for an ambulance, but the stressed and abrasive woman on the phone told them, bluntly, it would probably be better if they made their own way to A&E.

Segi stayed with his brother, keeping him talking and gently coaxing him away from sleep. In his battered state, another ride on the quad was out of the question, so they booked a corporate taxi. The black Benz pulled up fifteen minutes later and sent them a notification. Zaki was crying and wincing at every step as they carried him down the stairs. They got to the pavement in time to see the auto pull away. Some remote pilot, obviously not thrilled at the prospect of cleaning blood off expensive leather seats.

It was eight kilometres to the nearest hospital; the two closer hospitals had been closed due to cuts. Bouncing around in the trailer of a quad bike, it felt like fifty. Zaki had tried to be brave, but had cried out from time to time as they bumped over a pothole or swerved to avoid debris on the road. He had slipped into unconsciousness again, just before they arrived at the hospital.

The casualty waiting room was packed. It had the look and smell of a dishevelled and overcrowded ward. Small, concerned huddles stood around their supine charges who lay, covered in blankets or coats, stretched out across rows of repurposed chairs. There was nobody behind the reception desk. After ten minutes, Vikram found a passing nurse and grabbed her by the arm. She shook him off angrily, ignoring Anosh, who was still holding the unconscious Zaki, while sitting on the floor with his back to the waiting room wall.

Finally, after another hour, a doctor passed and looked at the pathetic vignette.

"What happened to the boy?"

"Compound fractures of the wrist and humorous, fractured skull, broken ribs. Possible fractured pelvis and internal bleeding," Vikram answered.

Anosh started at the final statement. He hadn't realised his son might be bleeding out, while they sat there on the grubby floor being treated like shit.

"Are you a doctor?"

"Yes."

"Let me take a look."

Anosh was expecting them to be led to a room or ward, but instead the doctor crouched down next to Zaki and began prodding and pinching. Zaki gave a shudder and cried out when the doctor touched his ribs on the right side, briefly coming back to consciousness.

"Okay, I'll try to find a bed. We really need to put him in the CAT scanner, but it's out of order. We can try to send him to Solungen," the doctor muttered, mostly talking to himself.

They spent another two hours on the floor before finally getting anything approaching modern medical treatment. The doctor used an old ultrasound machine. Anosh thought he recognised the type from when the boys were still residents of Ayşe's abdomen.

"What is this? You can't check for internal bleeding or set his arm with this thing!" Vikram shouted. He had pushed his way into the small office with Anosh. He was shaking now, furiously pointing at the yellowed plastic machine.

"That's what I thought when I first tried."

Every now and again, a sharp contour emerged from the chaos, but the screen showed nothing that Anosh could make any sense of.

"In fact, if you tweak the contrast and frequencies, and if you have a lot of practice... well, it's not perfect, but it's better than nothing," the doctor continued. He moved the wand over Zaki's chest and stomach for a few minutes before turning to the broken arm.

Then the examination was over. Zaki was still lying on the table, while the doctor laid out the options.

"I don't think there is any serious internal bleeding. It would have started to clot by now and collect in pools, but I can't see anything, so it's probably okay. I can set the humorous, but the wrist is smashed in too many places."

"Can't you pin it?" Vikram asked.

The doctor looked at Anosh. "I don't have an operating theatre. I don't have titanium pins. I have plaster and bandages, and I will do what I can. Do you understand?"

"This is ridiculous! You are a doctor and this is a hospital! Why can't you..." Vikram was losing his cool again.

"I will do my best with what I have," said the doctor. "Please keep quiet, or I will have to ask you to leave!"

"Okay, I understand. Please do what you can for my son." Anosh felt helpless, while boiling inside at the injustice that prevailed.

"I don't have a bed," said the doctor. "You can wait here until we need the room again, and I can find you a chair and a blanket and some cushions. You should stay here tonight in case he gets worse. I will be back to set the arm in the morning before I leave. Okay?"

Vikram left shortly after Anosh and Zaki were settled down onto a spare piece of floor in a long, packed corridor. It brought back memories of airports in snowstorms. Every available piece of floor had been taken. People had built little walls between the groups with suitcases and plastic bags. Cardboard boxes served as mattresses. A few eyes turned towards them as they staked out a space. Zaki was sleeping. They had given him Paramol for the pain. The prescription of generic over the counter painkillers for a child in Zaki's condition had nearly caused Vikram to flip out again.

Astonishingly, Anosh slept for a few minutes, despite the light, the coughing, farting, screaming, and lack of any form of comfort. He was surprised to discover it was 6 am, and the nurse and doctor had come to set the broken arm and wrist as best they could. Anosh looked at the translucent skin and huge black rings under the doctor's eyes and recognised this man had probably been working since the previous afternoon.

Zaki screamed as the doctor manipulated the two ends of his snapped upper arm and held them in place, while the nurse applied the bandages and plaster. The two worked efficiently and were soon done, finishing up by snipping and tying the loose bandage and then tidily packing away their rudimentary kit. Anosh, in a daze, thanked the doctor, who gave an exhausted nod.

"He should be okay. Looks like the concussion is not too bad. I'll be back on shift at eight tonight. Stay here 'til then, and I'll give him another examination."

Another nurse rushed up to the doctor. She pulled him away from them and directed him up the corridor. He sighed and followed, not even looking back to say goodbye, his shift clearly not quite over.

As Anosh watched them go, he felt claustrophobic—trapped here under the flickering blue strip lights. He tried as best he could to comfort his feverish, delirious son, while around him others were crying or dying.

Chapter 13 - Another World

The overseer's booth might once have been plush, but now it was frayed and grimy. Cigarette burns scarred the desk and carpet. Green and faded curtains were drawn across the grubby translucent windows. They could hear the machines through the heavy glass panes separating the office from the shop floor. Row upon row of rusty arms, drills and grabbers, a lunging mass of fading blue paint and rust. Shy, darting little creatures dodged amongst the dinosaurs. The furtive workers braved the crazy, deafening sea of moving robot arms to oil and tweak or to break up deadlocks when the priorities of the obsolete, primitive robots clashed, and they could not settle their own arguments.

The machines seemed mostly to be making electric bikes; flash-welding the tubes to brackets and housings for the super capacitors and batteries. Most of the tubular steel was piled up, waiting, but leaning prominently against the office wall were several of the heavy steel tubes made up in the familiar double triangle of a bike frame.

'No wonder the bikes need such powerful batteries; they're built like tanks,' Keith thought.

He was waiting to go through the paperwork with the site's Senior Fabrication Manager. The man turned out to be pale, with sunken eyes and a penchant for thick, silver jewellery. Keith had come in riding shotgun on the lorry that had delivered the batteries for the bikes—six hundred million ECUs of regulated high technology export, shipped in from Korea via Liverpool and then through the Holy Head tunnel and into the Dublin unregulated zone. He was not sure why he was here or what he had to offer that an admin-bot couldn't take care of.

A flicker in his mammalian peripheral vision, tuned to sudden splashes of red, made Keith turn towards the shop floor. The soundproofed windows blocked the screaming, but he watched a mob of bodies coagulate as the non-union oilers rushed to help one of their colleagues. Keith had turned toward the window in time to see the poor fellow being wrestled out of the grasp of a flailing mechanical arm. Blood was squirting out of his hand. The machine that had assaulted him rotated its arm above the throng and seemed to display proudly the bloody fingers it had torn loose and was still clutching greedily. The Fab-Manager turned away from the scene. Without comment, he went back to checking the paper invoice Keith had placed in front of him.

"How old is this stuff?" Keith waved through the glass.

"Thirty years or so… it's from Detroit."

"It's cheaper to pay all these guys and their medical settlements than upgrade to more human compatible automation?"

"The idiot is just clumsy. That's the second finger he's lost. Clumsy little Mulo, gives us a bad rep!"

"Lawsuits not an issue then?"

The manager looked up and, for the first time, made eye contact with Keith. He stared for a few seconds, but ignored the question.

"Here's your money," he said proffering the printout, signed and stamped.

Keith looked at the paper, and the money it represented, then back through the window towards the bloodied workers. The Fab-Manager watched him watching.

Backbones were a moral liability. The anarchic international melee that had replaced regulated globalisation was an environment much more suited to flexible bodied germs and parasites. The world was full of people and their crap, the oceans a toxic soup with plastic croutons, the coastline suffocated by hundred kilometre strips of overpopulated conurbation.

Keith was just trying to get by, get enough stuff to create a small local bubble of moral insulation. Like billions of others, he donated to tree-planting programmes, spent his money carefully, and hoarded his Impact Tokens; but after twelve months of working for BHJ, it was getting harder to spin a convincing inner narrative that painted him as anything other than one of the bad guys. Even here, on a simple visit to a factory pumping out electric bikes, he was exposed to the corporate abuse of the Have Nots. It even seemed a little touchy-feely for BHJ, a long way away from the usual environmental blackmail and computational brainwashing. Keith was surprised there were any angles to play in a commodity manufacturing enterprise. It seemed unlikely, but perhaps somewhere there was a division of BHJ that did real work.

Being socially responsible was expensive. Everybody had money these days, but money was worthless, unless you also had the Impact Tokens to spend it. The debts of nations had disappeared overnight with inflation wiping the slate clean, but the issuing of environment Impact Tokens was pegged to the state of the world's environment. Each person received a licence to pollute; a share of the total mess the UN decided was sustainable for that year. The cleaner and more sustainable the world, the more Tokens would be issued, but the trend was down. Things were still getting worse. Each year, fewer Tokens were issued.

Impact Tokens entered the economy as luxury vouchers. The managed poor and itinerant serfs resold their rations to the rich for money—which, at the lower levels of the social ladder, translated to food and shelter.

In many post-depression regimes, the poor received their government handouts in direct exchange for handing over their Impact Tokens. Wiley governments could then sell these in the international market for bullion, or cash them in to allow their archaic polluting public industry to plod on. Enforcement was sporadic and loopholes gaping.

Keith liked to think he represented what was left of the middle classes, a vanishingly thin strip of humanity, who found themselves sandwiched between the hordes of serfs, who were too poor to pollute, and the aristocracy, who still flew the world in their jets and chilled and heated their mansions with fossil fuels. He was rich by most standards, but the money he received was a multiple of the hours he worked, not like the oligarchs, board members, or politicians who received their tithe directly from the spigot.

Keith had seen enough to loathe the system and its benefactors, and he especially loathed himself as he accepted the grubby, crumpled receipt from the gaunt Fab-Manager who, one germ to another, nodded with smug understanding.

A few minutes later, Keith was sprinting across the car park through curtains of rain as the heavens opened and dumped a few million tons of water over the isle, guaranteeing its emerald epithet for the foreseeable future. Soaking wet, he jumped into one of the passenger seats and slapped the go button. The little plastic bubble pulled away, first crunching on the gravel, and then gliding off onto the autobahn. He turned up the heating fans and shut his eyes. He tried to sleep as the almost non-existent shell of plastic and rubber vibrated along the inside lane, taking him to yet another airport. His mind was not ready to relinquish its grip and kept springing back to the childish team-building nonsense that Ben had planned for the next few days offsite.

'Fucking Atlantis!' he thought to himself.

At the airport, he had disengaged his brain's higher functions and, selecting 'follow the dog' mode on his Spex, let the wagging tail of a virtual Jack Russell guide him to the Air Atlantis check-in desk.

The flights had only started up the previous month, and Ben had boasted that BHJ had a fantastic rate. Keith had read in a magazine that the island utopia was still more concept than concrete, and he half expected to be sleeping on bare floors without a roof. Ben would probably spin that as a chance to bond through adversity.

The flight was not so pleasant. Keith, jaded by dozens of flights in business class, was bored and uncomfortable after four hours, irate and demanding after ten, and numb and institutionalised after eighteen. In the same magazine, he had read the world's newest King was pumping money into high-altitude airships and hydrogen-burning hypersonic sub-orbital shuttles, but Air Atlantis currently consisted of two ageing airliners.

When he stepped onto the hot pavement outside the arrivals terminal of Atlantis International airport, it was misty with a prickle of warm drizzle condensing out of super saturated sea air, 10 pm and still twenty-five degrees centigrade. He could smell the salt and hear the gentle sloshing from the sea, just the other side of the wide road. Out on the horizon, several clusters of bright lights looked like oil platforms, but Keith knew they were the foundations for luxury pods of residences or hotels being built out in the shallow water surrounding Bäna Island.

After a few minutes, a taxi pulled up next to him. It was

a black London Cab, complete with a muttering cockney driver. Keith had wondered, for the first few minutes of the journey, if the cabbie was, in fact, a clever animatronic puppet installed to add flavour to the Atlantis experience. However, he decided, after several more kilometres, that the mix of casual racism and the proud recitation of his two daughters' achievements was probably genuine human banality, rather than carefully crafted cynical marketing.

The island was a massive construction site. Even the airport had only been a skeleton, with a few desks and minimal staff. Keith felt like he was behind the scenes during the construction of Disneyland. Seen from the air, as they approached, he could clearly make out the reclaimed land the runway had been built on and the scars in the tropical forest, where big projects were being carved out of wilderness. The cheerful cabbie was happy to act as a tour guide, but Keith just wanted to get to the hotel and veg out before the silliness of the next few days.

He paid the driver—bits issued from his BHJ corporate wallet travelling across tens of thousands of kilometres of fibre, careening from the earth to high orbit on coherent beams of quantum information and into the clearing accounts of Atlantis—the funds arriving with only a couple of seconds' delay in the cabbie's wallet.

"Cheers, enjoy Atlantis!" he called before pulling away onto the deserted road meandering back to the airport.

Keith couldn't imagine he would have a very busy night.

In the distance, behind the hotel's classical marble façade, Bäna, the semi-dormant volcano from which the island took its name, towered above the hills. It, too, was dotted with clusters of lights and, every now and again, it broadcast a massive rumble of distant thunder. Keith hoped it was only blasting and heavy construction, rather than the harbinger of a fiery end for them all. A gust drove in off the sea, forcing a trickle of water down his neck. He shuddered more at the intrusion than the cold and then started across the deserted little courtyard with his wheelie bag. So far, he had seen less than a dozen human beings since getting off the mostly empty flight.

Although he had never been to this hotel or chain before, his BHJ Sage—he was calling her Monica—had booked him a room, based upon obscure, yet apparently very clever, algorithms. His preferences, socially weighted recommendations, and other intangibles, were ostensibly factored in to ensure he was optimally allocated. Keith suspected it was weighted almost exclusively for cost saving. Here on Atlantis, everything was shiny and new, so hopefully it wouldn't get the chance to mess up Keith's sleep with a room above the dance floor or looking out onto a kitchen extractor fan.

The hotel had only opened the previous week. There was still an electrician in the lobby fitting light panels to the ceiling. A cursory glance suggested he was the only other physical person present.

Before the big brass and glass revolving door had stopped spinning, Keith was met by a receptionist on intercept course. She smiled engagingly at him as she glided across the marble floor, her feet slipping slightly as if on ice. She had a hint of an Asian slant to her perfect features, and she oozed the strange combination of nervous innocence and sexual availability, which were the traditional hallmarks of an Anime cartoon heroine. She would show up on the hotel bill as a business expense.

"Hello Keith," she fluttered, while adjusting her indecently short skirt. "Can I be of any assistance…?"

She was a graphical user interface created by the hotel's AI. She only existed on Keith's Spex and inside his brain, but that was enough to trick his glands and gonads. Infrared cameras sprinkled around the lobby had, no doubt, detected the slight tumescence, and the server had dutifully passed the information on to her software. She parted her lips slightly.

"You are already checked in; would you like me to show you the way to your room?"

The motorised luggage trolley, doing a perfect impression of being pushed by the virtual bellboy, followed them into the lift and the bellboy seemed to punch Keith's floor. During the short ascent, Keith caught the virtual bellboy checking the virtual receptionist's arse; the attention to detail was impressive. Keith was liking this Niato guy.

He told the bellboy he could have a tip if he would unpack the suitcases. The slouching youth looked convincingly pissed off and left with the trolley. The receptionist/hostess, who had been waiting outside Keith's door, moved aside to let the bellboy pass. She was very polite and waited for an invitation to enter. Keith was perfectly aware that asking her in would initiate the adult entertainment transaction, but he appreciated that his face was not being rubbed in it. He was being treated with some dignity, for a change, even while ordering up a quick fuck from a virtual whore.

He called over and invited her in. His Spex bleeped quietly and a confirmation notification hovered briefly before sliding into his peripheral vision. After gratefully accepting his credit card details, she stepped into the room and out of her dress. Keith had no special hardware with him; the hotel could provide it, but he had no intention of sharing a cybernetic vagina with an anonymous list of business-men. Instead, he would have to work on the principles of suspension of disbelief and self-sufficiency.

Even as she pointed to the bed, Keith could see she was frowning. He had been a bad boy. Still thinking too ra-tionally, he wondered how she picked up on his triggers. Was the room's camera and microphone network reading his physiological responses, or was she, or rather it, paying dubious BotNets to mine his tastes, based on the websites he visited and the books he bought?

She pulled her briefs into a T, and Keith stared transfixed as her soft virtual flesh welled up around the vertical axis of their sheer black material. She seemed to know him better than any real girlfriend ever had.

Four minutes later, it is nearly over; she is kneeling on Keith's bed, poised above him, just out of reach, encouraging him. A few more seconds and it is all too much; with an audible exclamation, Keith releases his tension. There seems to be a lot of it too. Great thick ropes of it shooting into the air, arcing like a Vegas fountain, indifferent to mundane concepts like gravity, and then splashing extravagantly over her perfect face and tits.

There is a pause as the universe sorts itself out, then she smiles, wipes herself down with her briefs and slips into her dress. She blows him a kiss as she leaves Keith to clean up the less-Herculean, non-virtual residues.

The next morning, he woke to the sun streaming into the room. He enjoyed its natural light. He delighted in the abstract whimsical patterns it made on the wall, as the rays were split into their component colours by the half-drunk glass of water by his bed.

A morning free of hangovers or vague troubling memories was a pleasant rarity for Keith. He called up Monica on his Spex and requested the headlines:

An earthquake in San Francisco, twelve dead.

A major storm in Bangladesh, which had broken through the dykes again, killing an undetermined number of people, expected to be in the tens of thousands.

Rebel fundamentalists in Yinchuan had sabotaged a nuclear reactor, causing millions of people to be evacuated and potentially polluting two thousand kilometres of the Yellow River.

Something in the broadcast stood out. Keith commanded his Spex to rewind and loop the last story, so he could look more closely at the images. A group of terrorists were posing in front of a smoking hole in the reactor's concrete apron. They were all waving RPG launchers and coil guns—millions of turns of super conducting wire driven by a couple of whooping great capacitors and powered by high-capacity batteries, they were capable of firing copper slugs through a tank. Keith recognised the barrels from yesterday's visit to the Irish factory, where they had been masquerading as bicycle crossbars. He could make a confident guess who had supplied the capacitors and batteries.

Bastards! So now BHJ had him gun-running for terrorists too! Fuck it!

He kicked off the duvet and stood up. With all contentment and optimism shattered, he was ready for another shitty day. Then he remembered! The morning was set aside for a data confidentiality training. This would be followed by a workshop on multi-cultural business practices for most of the afternoon, and finally they would finish the day with a team-building circle jerk. If Ben's previous on-sites were any indication, the night and early hours of the morning would be devoted to a massive piss-up.

'Fucking Ben!'

He got dressed and headed down in the gleaming brass and marble elevator to the patio, where breakfast was served. Keith couldn't see Ben, who was probably still in bed. The room seemed populated exclusively with the tanned young professionals Ben gathered to himself; lean bodies, smiling faces, loose morals. He was painfully aware of the grit at the corners of his eyes, the fur on his teeth, and the wad of fat lolling over the top of his trousers.

As he approached the breakfast buffet, Monica, ever helpful, informed him that his weight was trending above his two hundred day moving average, approaching an all-time high.

The hash browns and sausages no longer looked as succulent and enticing as they had a few seconds before.

***

Keith's Companion chirped, reminding him it was time to trot along like a good boy. He was still sitting in the breakfast room with the remnants of his third coffee, his bowl of bran flakes pushed back in disdain. In his current fragile mental state, he was not sure he could take the stupid waste-of-time sycophantic serial arse-kissing of the next few days.

He forced himself to summon some energy and asked Monica to check his calendar. After the onsite, he had another epic series of flights, followed by a joyful stint of debt collection for a corporate client at a group of farming collectives in Portugal. He had dealt with the farmers before. He knew they didn't have the money. They were three months behind on the payments for their EHW—electricity, heat, water—system, and the BHJ SLA demanded Keith carry out the threat he made last time he saw them. BHJ's client could much more easily use a remote Kill-Switch to shut down the system. One certificate revocation and the whole complicated setup would revert to an inert mass of metal and glass: algae turning foul, turbine rotors locking up and solar panels shorting out, but that was not the personal shakedown service BHJ prided itself on providing.

He knew he was not being sufficiently cynical. This thinking assumed a sort of honour amongst thieves, but human motives are a flowery fairy tale. Reality is a cold emotionless analysis that has calculated that sending Keith to deliver the news, in person, to a crowd of distraught farmers and crying children, would be better for future business.

The organisation he worked for possessed nothing like human sympathies.

He wandered out of the breakfast room, leaving his Companion on the table. He was still wearing his jeans and the hotel dressing gown. Some of the chirpy young executives paused their chattering and turned to watch the sad fat fuck in the flapping monogrammed terry towel robe. He imagined hands lifted to faces and excited hushed whispering, already propagating news of his putative meltdown. Only thirty-five, already jaded like a fifty-eight-year-old alcoholic nose-diving gonzo porno producer.

The doors to the breakfast room opened onto a little veranda. Keith's eyes were crusted with sleep gunk, so he took off his Spex to rub them, leaving his eyes naked for a change. He saw a rare and unadulterated view of his environment. A rustic dry stone wall, hung with flowering creepers, surrounded the veranda and a set of steps cut out of the rock led off from one corner to a beach below. A nasty extruded metal handrail tried to mess with the aesthetics, but when you add the beautiful view of cliffs, the waves, and the frolicking youths below, it was idyllic.

Let Ben and his little flock of robotic sycophants run through the motions of corporate responsibility without him. Keith decided to call in a sick day.

Skiving off was not as easy as it used to be. Monica, his pedantic intrusive company-issued agent, in a very literal sense, ran Keith's life. Appointments, notes, and contacts were just the surface. She knew him and, more importantly, she knew and understood every detail of his employment contract with BHJ. She knew where he was, where he should be, what he was eating and how often he was shitting it out again. If he was sick, she would call him a doctor, and if the doctor said he was not sick, she would tell him where his next appointment was, how long he had to get there—and, if he should miss the appointment, where the nearest exit was and when he could expect to be mailed his personnel belongings.

All this was passing through Keith's mind as he looked at the surf and the surfers scattering the beach. Somehow, his legs turned him around; he couldn't skip a morning and go surfing. They wouldn't fire him for that, but it would be a blip, a bonus burner, a promotion postponer. Yet, as he got back to his table and saw the Companion sitting smugly, blinking on the coffee-stained tablecloth, he knew he couldn't put up with Ben's crap today, either.

Two hours later, he had concocted a plan, changed into a pair of canvas shorts, and paid for a week of room and board in a less luxurious hotel along the beach. He drew out enough cash to keep him in food and beer for a few days. Sometimes, honesty is the best policy. The breakfast room was full of witnesses who would confirm he was, at most, a short stumble away from a full-on meltdown. So why not simply burn out for a while? In a couple of weeks, when he decided that perhaps he could take the bullshit again, before he was grilled by a company psychiatrist, he could subtly mention to Ben that all the blood on his hands from the illegal weapons he was complicit in dealing to violent sadistic international terrorists, must have pushed him over the edge, but he was better now and ready to get back to work, if that was all right.

So, he was back outside with his bags, five steps down from the veranda on a semi-concealed narrow stone landing, stooping down to smash his Companion to pieces, when a big, good-looking Asian guy came bouncing up the steps. Keith paused for a second, but from the frozen pose, it was clear what he was about to do. He shrugged, then, whacking the glass and aluminium Companion against the wall, watched the screen shatter satisfyingly into hundreds of pieces. Various arcane components scattered the surrounding shrubs and cactuses.

The guy didn't even break his stride, but bounded on. Passing Keith, he gave the high five sign and shouted, "Surf's up, dude."

Keith surprised himself by landing the palm slap response at short notice and headed on down to the beach, feeling cool. A few seconds later, he was back, grubbing through the grit for the solid-state storage, which he put in his pocket for a more thorough disposal later.

The sun had disappeared behind the big volcano half an hour before. Most surfers had come up the beach to be close to fires being gently coaxed into life there. The riders sat around chatting, surrounded by an irregular shell of boards jammed sharp end first into the sand and draped with wetsuits. Keith seemed to have chosen the little boutique hotel well; its beach was a surf Mecca.

After a morning of lying under the shade of a palm tree, a morning spent moving his hotel issue towel every thirty minutes to keep himself within its irregular splat of shade, Keith's hand-slapping friend had called him over to where a dozen tanned men and women were eating a lunch of melon and mango. He had taken the juicy segment of watermelon and, after a brief set of introductions, he considered their offer to lend him a surfboard.

The waves were gentle, the water clear, the sky blue. He accepted and then made a fool of himself for the rest of the day. Along the way, he had acquired a large board-inflicted bruise on the back of his head and plenty of scraped skin.

His exhaustion and aches at least felt honest. His Companion-smashing stunt had been re-told, giving him more kudos than his pale skin and flaccid belly might normally warrant in such circles. The burly Asian guy called himself Nick. He was a big bouncy bloke, who communicated with an excessive amount of backslapping. Contrary to Keith's initial impressions, he was not a trustafarian stoner. Rather, he described himself as an anarchist and CEO. He was coy about what his company did, but mentioned synthetic ecosystem design and photic zone fabrication of self-assembling calcium carbonate structures. Without his

Companion or Spex, the words were meaningless to Keith.

'Damn, he's cool!' Keith thought, enjoying a little man crush.

Yesterday, he would have said smug and narcissistic, but today, having raised his middle finger to the man, he wanted to be a surfer anarchist, too.

They were sitting cross-legged on the beach, around a fire of driftwood, drinking from big brown bottles of beer cooled by the Pacific surf. They were passing around a joint.

'Okay, so he is a stoner,' Keith internally corrected himself.

"Hey, good progress out there today, bud!" said one of the entourage, passing Keith the joint.

"Ha! Thanks. No. Come on. I was terrible, right?"

"Yeah, but you tried and that's what makes the difference in the end. Stick with it," the chap said with a laugh.

"Sure. Will do."

"So what do you do, man?"

"Did. You mean, what *did* he do? You quit. Right?" asked Nick.

"Well, let's just say I'm taking a couple of days to think about my future."

"Right, so what *did* you do?" the same guy asked again. Keith had forgotten his name and, without his augmentation, he was crap at remembering them.

"Oh, you know, PR, B to B, and B to C liaison stuff…"

"Monkey in a suit, right? Grease on the wheels of the corporate juggernaut? I know the type. Wild youth. Unfocused talent. Flexible moral character…" Nick interrupted.

Some of the others stopped their own conversations or leant in to listen. Nick was speaking. Not chatting or joshing, but speaking, and when Nick spoke the others listened. Or, as Nick had to remind a few in the past, they fuck off.

Keith had originally thought these guys were a bunch of waster friends with rich daddies on holiday, but Nick had authority. This was his company. Sure, they were friends, but more than that, they were a team, and this was work. If this was their onsite, it was better than the tedious training courses and seminars Ben scheduled as a flimsy justification for flying everybody out for a massive piss-up.

Earlier, while the fires were being lit, Nick had continued unambiguously to lay down the law: Keith was welcome to hang out, borrow a board, catch waves, but some of the stuff they might talk about was privileged; and, if Keith hung, he would be implicitly agreeing to a blanket non-disclosure agreement. From a journalistic point of view, everything was off the record. Keith had protested at that point that he wasn't a journalist, but Nick had ignored him, insisting everybody with Spex was a journalist. He didn't want there to be any confusion later when Nick sued the shit out of BHJ for corporate espionage. Everything said by any member of the group was off the record, unless explicitly stated otherwise, and then only for the agreed points.

Sitting nearby, an attractive Asian female with vibrant strawberry-blonde hair, wearing a pink and khaki one-piece, was recording the conversation on a small waterproof Companion.

"Yeah, most of that is true. I'm not keen on the flexible moral character stuff though. But it's probably true. Fuck it, right? A man's got to survive somehow," Keith said, pausing to suck on the spliff.

"Wrong!" replied Nick. "You're not stupid, so you're not innocent. If your flexible morals hurt people, then they hurt people, period. People are hurt, and that's bad, so it's not fuck it. You need to do better than that, or it's fuck you, I'm afraid."

Keith's head was spinning from the Ganja and beer, and he wasn't sure what had just happened to the friendly après surf beer and smoke. Things had seemed to be going so well, and now they were going downhill fast.

"What? Slow down. I don't know what you think I do, but I'm just a bloody pawn, a runner. Take this to there, collect that, just shit. Tedious shit."

"Oh, right, the Nuremburg defence. 'I was just following orders,' right?" said Nick.

"Oh, fuck you!" Keith rocked to his feet. "I don't need this shit. Look, when I was a kid, maybe I thought I could change the world, but nobody gives a shit. To get anything done, you need to change all the selfish ignorant people first. It didn't take a genius to work out that that one was never gonna fucking fly. But you've got to eat, so you get a job. I don't want to burst your bubble, Nick, but it's not all beaches and sexy secretaries out there."

The secretary started to protest, but was silenced by a wave from Nick as Keith continued.

"It's shit. Blood and shit and that's the way it always was and always will be. So FUCK YOU. Fuck you all. I'm going to fucking bed."

"Easy tiger," said Nick, standing and grabbing Keith's arm as he turned to leave.

Keith was pissed, stoned, and filled with a powerful self-loathing. Enraged by the goading, he reacted wildly to Nick's fingers on his arm. He lashed out, scything his fist around in a huge swinging arc. More by luck than design, he landed the punch in the middle of Nick's big, smiling face—roughly in the nose area, judging by the little explosion of blood.

Keith was not exactly sure what happened next. Most of the others were rushing up to encircle their captain, but he noticed the secretary again, still in the one-piece swimming costume, but now with a khaki denim jacket framing her flat stomach and curvaceous upper body. She wedged herself between Keith and Nick, then pirouetted around, dragging Keith to the ground, while doing something complex with his arm, which resulted in her sitting on his back, crushing his face in the sand with her legs scissoring his neck. It was all fast and calm. He couldn't breathe. He could barely move. One arm was trapped under him. The other was drawn behind his back. Without fuss, she was choking him gently into unconsciousness with her thighs.

It was quite intimate. He hoped she wouldn't kill him.

When he opened his eyes again, he saw stars and the moon. He was lying in the warm sand, with khaki one-piece sitting on a log a couple of metres away on the other side of the fire. She was looking away from him and out towards the surf, but presumably she was still watching him out of the corner of her eye, vigilant for any sudden moves. He decided to lie there for a while and sort his head. She didn't seem to be in any hurry, either.

Eventually, he propped himself up onto his elbows. "Sexy secretary and scary assassin, isn't it?"

She looked around. "You're confused. I'm just the life guard. You're the corporate fascist bully boy."

"Oh Jesus, here we go again. I am a dogsbody, underpaid and overworked. Crap benefits. No job security. No executive capacity. It's a shit job."

Nick wandered into Keith's field of vision with a bottle of beer pressed to the side of his nose. He must have been sitting or standing somewhere behind Keith.

"Still *is* and not *was* though?" he asked.

"Sorry about the nose, Nick. I think you touched a nerve with your little character assassination. Why are you so interested in what I do? Thinking about offering me a new job or something?"

"Nope, we don't have any opportunities at the moment, but I'm always on the lookout for talent; you never know. I could tone down the lectures if I knew for sure you were an ex, rather than operational, corporate goon and spy."

"Spy? Is that what all this is about? I'm not a fucking spy! I got up this morning and pulled a sicky, because I couldn't handle another day of bullshit from my boss. I came down to the beach to chill, met a couple of nice people." Keith's eyes, unbidden, glanced over to khaki one-piece. "I had a beer and then seem to have been ambushed by a crack deep cover left-wing political debating squad."

"Ha!" Nick laughed. "Okay bud, sorry. No more politics. You can hang with us if you want, but forget the sucker punches or I'll let Dee really fuck you up next time."

"Fair enough. How long was I out?"

Dee looked down to him from the other side of the fire. "Five minutes or so. I hardly had to touch you, though. Mostly it was the drugs and booze and general fatigue that took you under. Not been sleeping too well lately?"

"How'd you guess? And before you ask: Yes, it is my guilty conscience keeping me awake at night. Got another cold one there, Nick? I seem to have dropped my last one somehow."

He struggled up and joined the circle around the fire. The guy sitting next to him on the log passed along a new beer and said, "A lot of people react to him like that. He likes to pick at scabs. Don't worry about it. You're not the first bloke to smack him one. That's mostly what he keeps Dee around for."

***

Keith stood a little back from the edge of the precipice. He felt like a painful union between a bat and a penguin. He reached his arm around to the back of his suit. He flapped his elbows to shake the folds of cloth out of the way, and his fingers found the tennis ball-sized lozenge snuggling between his shoulder blades. For good measure, he gave it a tug to make sure it was still firmly attached to his harness.

Over the past few hours, what had already seemed like a dubious idea when they discussed it the night before had acquired all the characteristics of a fever dream. Head still groggy, he had been dragged away from his half-drunk breakfast coffee and cajoled up onto an antique coach with scuffed faux leather seats and a wood-patterned linoleum aisle. The justification for the excessive good luck paraphernalia dangling from the mirror and festooned across the dash became clear as soon as the old coach juddered forward and began the long precarious climb up the slow motion landslide comically masquerading as a road. Forty minutes after stepping off the coach, having left behind the smelly, overheated engine, he saw the spectacular jungle-fringed valley dropping away into the mist before them and finally grasped the magnitude of his situation.

"It's easy as falling off a log," Dee said, grinning at him before leaping after the others, who had already taken leave of their senses and parted company with the ground. Keith stayed rooted to the big, solid, safely grounded boulder the others had just left. He looked down past the overhang; Dee, arms and legs spread like a flying squirrel, was hurtling past jagged rocks towards the tops of the jungle trees seven hundred metres below. Way in front, Nick—or Nate-O, as some of the others called him—was levelling out of his dive. He and a couple of the others had suits with big overlapping carbon fibre scales attached to an elegant arrangement of levers across their backs. Nick partially unfurled his black, death-angel wing extensions and, scrubbing speed, climbed up from the treetops.

The previous evening, following the tussle on the beach, they had been talking about their plans for the next day. Nick and the others would be guiding a group of business men on an unforgettable adventure, demoing a new product —namely, the twelve-square metres of graphene nano-cloth that Keith was wearing packed into the tiny cylinder on his back. A small, but capable, flight computer controlled the electroactive risers and, when required, tiny rockets would rip the chute from its protective bubble. Feeling slightly left out and intending to try to boost his cred a little, Keith had mentioned that, while at school, he had done a parachute jump once. Nick had immediately perked up, spearing him with his feverish will. He insisted Keith come with them on the base-jumping escapade. Conscious of Dee sitting across the table watching, Keith had agreed.

"The auto-chute will open if there is any danger, and it will guide you in. It's perfectly safe," they had told him ten minutes earlier during a terrifyingly informal safety presentation.

The chute was small enough to be worn by the paranoid on commercial flights or to provide a modicum of safety to the suicidal adventurist when engaged in extreme sports. Nick had gone to great lengths to explain its features. Thinking back to the conversation, Keith thought it had sounded very technical and complicated, when perhaps, if he had been choosing a parachute for himself, simple and reliable might be the features he would prioritise.

His procrastinating reverie was broken by an enthusiastic exclamation: "Fucking hell! Looks like you are feeling better, hey Keith?"

He turned towards the familiar voice and saw Ben and his entourage disembarking from a much nicer white coach. It must have pulled silently into the clearing behind them. Its sleek form was streaked with reddish mud from the climb up from the coast. Keith's stomach lurched as he realised these must be the corporate customers Nick had meant.

"Busted!" mentioned one of Ben's drones, helpfully raising his hand for a high five from Ben that never arrived.

Experimental parachutes, reckless instructors, and the real possibility he would be bounced and abraded from the rocks on the way down, until he was merely a sinewy collection of organs and shattered limbs slapping and sliding towards the jungle far below, were all mere irritations, compared to this new source of ultimate ironic misery.

"Fuck," Keith muttered under his breath.

The prospect of leaping off the edge was looking like the lesser of two evils. Before Ben could say anything else, with a massive surge of will, he insisted to himself there was the calm surface of a swimming pool just over the edge. Willing himself to believe in the water a few metres below, against the advice of all his instincts, he performed a clumsy dive.

He is tumbling. The wall of the cliff is a blur, indifferent to the screaming human hurtling past it.

'Why isn't the FUCKING chute opening?' he thinks, yelling incoherently.

Some primal mammalian instincts assert themselves. He extends an arm. The tumbling slows, but then reverses. He opens his legs and the webbing between them catches the air and pitches him into a headfirst dive. Three eternal seconds of experimentation later and Keith has managed to stop spinning about his axis. His fall can now be generously described as a very steep and suicidal glide. The flight computer has been optimistically plotting scenarios that do not end with his mashed body, but it can no longer see any branches of its simulation tree that do not involve bits of bone and pints of blood splashed around the boulders of the riverbed a hundred metres below.

The chute deploys perfectly and then, apparently without transition, Keith is standing in a small stream, his translucent black parachute collapsing around him.

He briefly wonders why it smells of shit here, thinking it improbable and ironic that, given the large expanse of riverbed, the computer should land him on a large pile of fresh turd. Then, a more likely explanation occurs to him and he begins to struggle out of his soiled suit before the others arrive.

"Fucking ACE!" yelled Ben twenty minutes later. He had crashed into the stream a dozen metres away.

Keith emerged from behind the boulder where he had been rinsing stubborn chunks from the seams of his suit. Ben had already unzipped his leg flap in the middle and wrapped the two sections around his legs, so he didn't have to hobble like a convict.

"Ah, shat yourself I see."

"Fuck off Ben," Keith suggested.

"Easy Keith. Don't forget you work for me. So let me guess; you felt a bit better and thought that a spot of base jumping might be just the thing to help you convalesce?"

Keith saw Nick and Dee trudging back up the stream. Dee was holding the scrunched-up ball of her chute. Nick was empty-handed. Keith would later watch the video of him using his huge strap-on wings to scrub most of his speed and then barefoot water ski to a halt across a calm pool in the river, effortlessly jogging up onto the sandy beach in one final heroic flourish.

Ben saw them coming and did a comical double take. Keith assumed he was just ogling the beautiful Dee, but Ben was suddenly deadly serious and gave Keith a curious look, pressing pause on any conversation.

"Mr Munisai, your highness, what a pleasure. I didn't expect to be lucky enough to have the honour of meeting you!" Ben said, all traces of cockney rough edges gone from his voice. He extended his hand for a shake. Nick gave it a horizontal double slap surfer style.

"Hey! And no need to be formal. I am just Niato, or Nick,"

he said, giving Keith a slightly guilty shrug.

"Okay, cool, well it's still an honour. Shall we go again?" Ben asked, gesturing towards the harness swinging gently from an invisible filament back at the cliff.

"Sure. Did you enjoy yourself?" Niato asked.

"Yeah! Amazing. I want to try it with those wings of yours next," said Ben.

"Sorry, no can do. After a couple of hundred hours in a simulator, maybe you can give them a go out of a plane. Way too dangerous close to the ground for a beginner. Trust the chute; it knows best and is an expert pilot."

"Yea, whatever. Maybe next year, right?"

"It's a deal," Niato answered with an apparently genuine smile.

Ben stepped into the harness and clipped himself on. At some invisible signal, the sling accelerated up towards the top of the cliff. A few minutes later, the harness came down again. By then, more of the others were returning and queuing up to ascend the cliff for another hit of adrenaline.

"You going again Keith?" Niato asked.

Keith was running over the previous day and night, scanning his internal narrative for all the times he had embarrassed himself or insulted the world's most popular Royal. Plenty of drunken goofs arrayed themselves for inspection, but top of the list was definitely punching the

King in the face.

"Sure," he responded with a rictus grin slicing his face in two.

The 'rope' was so unfeasibly thin that it was dangerous to touch anywhere other than on the specially padded regions. The ground was quickly a long way away. Keith was lofted up the cliff in a series of massive sickening swings. He decided this was even more terrifying than the way down. Then he remembered the sphincter loosening terror of the descent.

At the top, an instructor fitted him with a new chute. The old one was still lying below, scrunched up into its pouch. It could not be re-folded by hand and would be sent back to the Fab for refurbishment and re-packing. Keith noticed a few of this group were wearing chunky rocket boots. These flyers were so proficient, they didn't need chutes to land; they only wore them for last-ditch safety. Wings and jet boots worked together to create a dynamic that brought their landing speed down below a bone-shattering hurtle. Apparently, only Niato had mastered the water-skiing swoop landing.

Ben and Keith, who were absolute beginners, weren't trusted with rocket boots or wings. They didn't have the option to try a landing yet, relying instead on the flight computer to pull their chutes fifty metres from the ground.

"How was that then?" asked another of Niato's crew.

"Yeah, better than I expected. Quite fun actually." Keith thought he had just managed to keep the terror out of his voice.

"Gonna try not to shit your pants again this time?" enquired Ben.

Keith glanced over at Dee, but thankfully, she didn't seem to have heard.

"Fuck off Ben!" Keith whispered.

They were all piling off the edge again, like a group of lemmings. Keith copied one of the others, leaping away from the cliff with arms out in a T shape. He was actually gliding. The stones whipping by below gave testament to his lateral motion, but before he could really get used to the sensation, his chute exploded away from his back. Ben, who must have been dangerously close behind, flashed by whooping. His chute opened a few metres in front of Keith.

"Beer?" Ben asked a few minutes later.

"You don't think maybe we should stay sober for this?"

"Oh, you're ill. I forgot. Whatever. I'm having one."

They walked back to the little camp at the base of the cliff and sat down in a patch of sun. The others were slowly coming back from a series of longer glides.

"Ah, that's the stuff." Ben laughed, taking a second chug. "You really are a tosser, Keith. You know that? You get a chance to rub shoulders with a real player, and you don't even recognise him. Such. A. Tosser!"

"For Christ's sake, Ben. Can you just give it a rest for a couple of minutes?"

"You're not really having a midlife crisis are you?"

"Ben, I'm not sure I can do this anymore."

"Hey Dee!" Ben shouted. "My boy Keith here needs to sort his head out. How about a bit of sexual healing?"

Dee looked at Keith, whose face was frozen in horror. She tipped her head to the side and gave Ben a bored look.

"He's not really my type," she replied, making light of the embarrassing question.

Keith knew his ears and cheeks were lighting up, but he tried to keep a lid on the murderous impulses jogging around his body. He felt his hands and jaws clench.

"Ben, what the fuck is wrong with you? We're not fucking twelve anymore."

Ben grinned and went over to give him a big cuddle, followed by a knuckle rubbing on the head. Keith tried to fight him off weakly, but this only seemed to encourage him. In the end, Keith stood up, got a hand under Ben's chin, and forced him away.

"Okay, that's it. I have had it. You don't get the message do you... FUCK. OFF!"

Ben stumbled back from the shove and got his legs tangled

up in a chair. Falling over a table, he crashed to the floor, a cascade of spilt beer pouring onto his head. He rolled over and thrashed back to his feet, and then kicked the offending chair across the wooden deck.

"Well in that case, fucking resignation fucking accepted," said Ben. "You can go back to waiting tables or selling your arse on Kings Cross for all I care. You ungrateful prick!"

"God, I fucking hate you!"

'Everything that is old is new again', Anosh thought with a smile.

His fingers tapped on the screen of an upcycled Companion. The austere, unadorned, text-heavy pages of the auction site had conjured a wash of happy nostalgia for a simpler time of naive images and text laid out like a picture book, passive and unassertive, content to be consumed at your leisure. Anosh was old enough to remember the old Web, when it had been a happy-go-lucky youth, before gamification and cynical click bait had remade it into a machine for turning out laboratory pigeons. But youth had jaded and morphed the internet into a narcissistic nymphomaniac. Browsing became a battle of wills as she begged and demanded—with mascara-streaked eyes—that you click the blinking shit away before any diluted morsels of gratification were reluctantly granted.

The transformation had been driven by the need for revenue. Sites had been stuffed with pseudo-intelligence for real time behaviour monitoring, lifeless logic allowing algorithms to judge from your actions the most effective messages and crude attention-stealing gambits. In a race to the bottom, the Web had become a jungle of malicious code-exploiting primate reward circuits to extort attention. Surfers were addicts, captivated by flashing lights and a constant stream of grinding genitals plastered across their multitude screens. Junkies, hooked by their need for the next micro reward.

Pecking - posting; liking; sharing; clicking.

It had happened slowly. Anosh recalled each new affront: needy sites that begged you not to leave, content spread thinly across dozens of advert-saturated pages, headlines eerily specific and resonant with ideas you may never have fully formulated. There was no privacy, even inside your own mind. Desire was teased from the subconscious by cold psychological models running on server farms measured in acres. They were fed with bulk data from a billion user habits and tuned with the latest academic research.

There was so much data that the expert systems came to know you better than you knew yourself; the way you moved your mouse over links before clicking, what you clicked when you were drunk, what you click after being shown X or Y, each byte further refining the caged homunculus they were building until they had your soul in a bottle.

The final metamorphosis into whatever the end-stage internet would have looked like had been interrupted when the collapse had crashed the system. Visitors had stopped spending; adverts stopped making money. Pages died, one after another. At the same time, a black hole of debt was sucking liquidity out of the economy, and great chunks of infrastructure were going dark as the companies that owned them sunk into financial oblivion. Vast clicking, whirring data centres became silent. The internet shrivelled back towards its mushy stump.

After a few winters without food and power, governments had gotten their shit together. They teamed up to create a surreal narrative that left Kafka behind and took economics deep into Escher territory. The translucent undead economy was pushed out onto the stage, with a shot of adrenaline in its arse and forced to sing one last time.

Society rebooted, but recovery was fragile; unrest and malcontent could not be allowed to disrupt their first faltering steps. Anger and betrayal needed to be calmed and hot flows of emotion redirected. Web marketers stepped up to the plate. Expertise at manipulating sentiment and brand loyalty let them take the old Synthetic Cognition algorithms and repurpose them. Expert systems were redeployed from creating click-bait advertorial content, to churning out socially resonant pacification propaganda. The internet surged back to life, but the optimism was gone. The eclectic, irreverent, mix of ideas had been replaced by a cloying, warm, all-embracing flood of subliminal, multi-channel propaganda in the familiar model of Telenovela daytime TV.

Most people allowed it to wash over them, to numb thought and pain, but for others, annoying webpages had gone from being intrusive to sinister. They would not forget the dark days of riots and the mass shootings when the governments had shown how far they would go to hold on to power. For these people, the low bandwidth Mesh was the answer, and they were happy to put up with its 90s ASCII aesthetic in return for keeping their heads free of synthetic mimetic viruses.

Pace of change was exceeding elasticity of mind. Ayşe didn't have Anosh's techno-utopian dreams. Instead, for her, and millions of others suffering from the epidemic of future-shock, the Caliphate's romantic glow beckoned, its Islamic nostalgia a refuge from the craziness. The Caliph's pleas for human dignity and his sermons of simplicity and moderation were a beacon, beckoning a growing chunk of disenfranchised humanity.

There were worse places in the world to be than moderately prosperous Dusselstadt—the UK, where Anosh had grown up, seemed to be unselfconsciously modelling itself on an RBC production of Orwell's *1994*. What was left of America, following its second civil war, had become a perpetual hillbilly cannibal cook-off. Much of Asia was a turmoil of ethnic conflict, civil war, and religious terrorism—but Ayşe, at some deep level beyond rationality, had wanted to leave, and Anosh had realised he could do nothing to change her mind.

Until now, the expanding amoeba that was the Caliphate had always sounded romantic and foreign and, at least to him, comfortably far away. His parents had left Iran in the seventies. They had fled to Prussia and became resolute atheists. They worked hard to integrate into their new home, while bringing up their three sons to share their perspectives on religion and freedom. He knew that, if his parents were alive, they would be horrified he was even thinking of making the return trip fifty years later.

Something in Ayşe had snapped while she powerlessly watched Zaki heal as a cripple. The Mesh was full of similar stories of distraught parents bemoaning the impotent State. Anosh felt like he had lost both—first, his innocent happy boy, then his wife, as he watched Ayşe get sucked into the Mesh's vast crystal maze of threads. She became confused and disorientated amongst the recriminations, blatant trolling, childish *griefing*, and the Forward propaganda. Increasingly, though, she had found clarity in the warm, measured, and reassuring words of the mullahs. Anosh tried to point out this was also propaganda, but she had grabbed onto an idea; and, trying to prise it from her grip

228

would probably have destroyed her, and it would certainly have torn the family apart.

Europe's generation-long War on Terror had created the Jihad in its many flavours. Forged in the fires of hate, it was anger personified and not a political movement with any real coherent policy. The recession, depression, and collapse left their enemy broken, stumbling around, geriatric and confused, lost, unable to remember how and why they had become bogged down in the dusty dessert.

Attacking the mighty infidel, so reduced, looked petty. The justification for war became less clear and moderate voices had risen to positions of power across the Byzantine mess of factions, fronts, rogue states, and cells that had formed at the leading edge of the Jihad.

Vibrant student protests and a colourful bright-eyed message of change and human dignity had lent an air of youthful panache to the struggle. Eventually, a legitimacy had been established that had tempted political heavy hitters, regardless of original inclination, away from their old employers. The groundswell of public opinion drew in spin doctors and campaign managers. Finally, they had a cause they could unite behind with popular slogans, strong on traditional values.

With the cream of the world's political conductors running the campaigns, the incoherent choppy video uploads of previous decades were expunged. Islam would no longer be making its points against a backdrop of beheading and terror. The focus was now a message of humanity and peace, respect and dignity. It was a message that resonated not just across the Middle East, Nusantara, and Fas, but also in London, Solungen, and a million impoverished, marginalised households across the globe.

If there was an enemy of Islam now, it was Idolatry.

"Man commits idolatry whenever he honours and reveres a created form in place of God," Ayşe had explained to Anosh, out of the blue one morning.

Corporations were the new false gods worshiped by the infidel media and politicians. They were the instruments of Satan with an anti-human agenda of accumulating Mammon at the expense of all God had created. They had become imbued with rights and freedoms, beyond those enjoyed by ninety per cent of humanity.

"Idolatry is worse than genocide," she had insisted.

Anosh rests for a few moments in the shade of an ancient gnarly oak tree, remembering their last few months together in Prussia.

Ayşe and the boys had been Catholic, at least on paper, as Ayşe had paid her church tax each year. She persisted in this, despite Anosh's gentle suggestion it was a waste of money and, frankly, morally suspect. She didn't profess to have any religious inclination—or, at least, she hadn't until Zaki's beating.

Fear and murder and, finally, the vicious attack on her oldest son had cracked something inside her. The vague cognitive dissonance on matters of religion she had always displayed—the cause of many earnest and endearing discussions when they first met, and the odd recurring repetitive argument ever since—all these positions had metamorphosed into a desperate fervent belief.

As Ayşe had subscribed to channels and joined forums, Anosh found there were growing blind spots he could not approach. If the conversation encroached on these taboos, they would argue—Ayşe becoming defensive and, ultimately, closing him out. The children were confused, but Anosh wouldn't stand between them and their mother for fear it would create a split in the family. Ayşe had no such qualms; powered by a righteous conviction, she was saving their souls. She followed the advice of her new online friends, preparing the boys for their conversion to Islam.

He unslings his rucksack and pulls the water bottle from its side pocket, taking a suck of warm water and checking his watch. There is still a long way to go, but he has time.

Ayşe had gathered the two boys to her. Zaki sat, contorted and uncomfortable, on the sofa beside her, while Segi sat on the floor and leant against her legs. On her Companion, she was viewing the image of a worryingly young bearded mullah, probably in a call centre somewhere, his upper body partially obscuring the white Arabic script on the green flag behind him.

Anosh had tried one last time to convince her to stop, while she was uploading pictures of the boys' newly circumcised penises. His pleas went unheard as Ayşe continued with her obsessive preoccupations.

The bearded man guided them through the scripted process.

"Ash-hadu an la ilaha ill Allah," they each said. "I bear witness there is no god but Allah."

Anosh hadn't been able to join them. It would have felt like a betrayal to his parents, knowing they had given up so much to spirit him out of Iran as a baby. They had risked their lives, so he might have the chance to grow up free from the suffocating, irrational intrusions into private life. He had also been convinced that Ayşe would, ultimately, see sense before taking the final step.

What hurt the most was that, as she continued to make plans, she hadn't seemed to mind he wouldn't be joining them. The space in her life he had inhabited had closed somehow.

"Ash-hadu ana Muhammad ar-rasullallah." "I bear witness that Muhammad is the Messenger of Allah".

Then they had showered, washing away their old sins to emerge, reborn. The mullah, showing emotion for the first time, welcomed them to the faith. Whether his smile indicated pious joy or cynical satisfaction at moving three souls closer to his monthly sales KPI was a matter of perspective. He sent them their certificates of Islam as PDFs, complete with biometric face and fingerprint data hashed and signed with the Caliphate's certificate. If they ever made it into the Caliphate, these would be exchanged for passports.

Vicious thorns infest the dry scrub and, although he hasn't seen any, he walks in constant fear of disturbing venomous snakes. He makes his way between ancient cedar trees, across a landscape of ridges and gullies, scattered with geometric ochre boulders. The Osmanian border is still six kilometres away, according to his Companion, and the dots representing his wife and kids are a further four kilometres beyond that. He hopes they will be waiting for him, with Aloe Vera for his bites and a big flask of chilled water to assuage his intense thirst.

Despite a constant seething turmoil of bewildered anger, Anosh had helped Ayşe trawl the Caliphate sites dedicated to guiding new converts and potential immigrés through the process. He had nudged her towards Osmaniye, rather than Durrani or Irak. Osmaniye had retained its own identity, resisting political homogenisation. It had also always fed and watered its children. According to the Mesh, it was one of the few countries on the planet with a net surplus of food. Global warming had made summers fierce, but had also increased the rainfall; rivers and reservoirs were full.

Even back then, he would have admitted the pastoral Arcadian life they were researching had appeal.

He swats at a massive horsefly making a meal of his arm and pushes on, wondering, not for the first or the last time, what the hell he had been thinking.

The Osmani weren't messing around at their borders, though. Landing unannounced on the Osmanian coast would most likely lead to unceremonious expulsion, if you were lucky, or direct exclusion from the land of the living, if you were not.

The family had parted company in Venice, and Anosh had felt as if parts of his body were being torn away. To say he bitterly regretted sticking to his principles was like saying a horsefly bite on the elbow itched a little.

He had been verging on the hysterical as his wife and sons had boarded an impossibly crowded ferry to Izmir. He had watched its propellers churn the puce water as it inched way from the quay. He was sobbing as it moved out into the Giudecca Canal and was lost; just one more vessel amongst the dozens coming and going.

With the dread of loss curled like a cold worm in his stomach, he had dragged himself back to the bus station for his lonely trip home to Dusselstadt. He knew that, with their new documents, Ayşe and the kids should have a smooth journey to what he was slowly coming round to believing might be a better life; but still, it had still felt as though he was dying, permanently losing all that really mattered to him.

He had managed to live for ten weeks alone before giving in. The ninth summer in the old printers should have delivered on all their investments of fixing, renovating, and re-inventing. The garden on the roof was established; Anosh enjoyed daily plates of sweet tomatoes and rocket. The Algal-solar-ponics was churning out litres of nutritious green slime that dried to make a crunchy wafer that was fishy and unpleasant, but nutritious. He spent his evenings sitting alone or drinking with and boring anybody who would listen to his emotional monologs. These all reduced down to an irrational hope that Ayşe would reconsider and miraculously reappear with his sons. Eventually, though, the glimpses of their lives he received via messages painted an increasingly rosy picture. He was moved to give up on keeping the nest warm and made preparations to follow after them.

Unfortunately, the Caliph was no longer offering web-based religious conversion and assisted immigration. Tens of thousands had applied and then made the pilgrimage to start a better life of meaning, but the quota had been reached, and the doors had been closed for this year. Without an official invitation, it would be much harder to go East. There were, however, always ways.

He sold their home to one of Vikram's wife's brothers, confident he could trust the family to continue paying him the MeshCoin they had agreed each month. The price was impossibly cheap, but the down payment would be enough to grease a few palms on the way. MeshCoins were supposed to be just as widely used in the Caliphate.

Information was free. Whether you were building a chicken coop, learning to safely identify mushrooms, or finding a coyote to smuggle you past the borders of a reanimated thirteenth-century oriental empire, you looked on the Mesh.

Following instructions and helpful step-by-step guides, he had hustled and bribed his way onto a ship in Greece bound for Port Said. By paying one of the crew for a few megabytes of data, he could keep up his spirits, messaging with his family as the old diesel-soaked passenger ferry inched its way across the Mediterranean.

According to plan, he had been immediately arrested, before even stepping off the boat in Egypt. Not mentioned in any of the 'walkthroughs', though, was the inconvenience of spending a week in a filthy camp of bare urine-scented concrete dorms and ragged tents, before getting a chance to demonstrate to the stone-faced military police that he had the coins required to bribe them. Probably, they let all the soft-looking virgins stew for a while as an incentive to offer an adequate bribe. He would update the Wiki page for the benefit of future users when he was settled. Eventually, after paying atrocious amounts of money to compensate for his lack of Islamic identification papers, he made it to the start of a huge, chaotic, jostling, multi-day queue to board a boat to Mersin. Each passenger seemed to have a better excuse than the last for why they needed to cut in.

Without the Wikis and walkthroughs, Anosh would probably never have made it out of Europe, but he would certainly never have considered getting off the overloaded boat with his goal so tantalisingly close. A finger of Kurdistan reached down to the Mediterranean at Latakia, sandwiched between Syria and Osmaniye. Kurdistan was a formal part of the sprawling Caliphate; in fact, it owed its very existence to the recognition it had been granted by the first Caliph, but old frictions persisted. This made the relationship between the two neighbours rather uncomfortable and diplomacy tortuous. It also meant, while the borders were officially closed, there was a need, and therefore a market, for unofficial border crossings.

At least, that is what the Mesh had led Anosh to believe. As a result, he had found himself a Kurdish Coyote before leaving Prussia and, if things were still on track, the smudge of smoke across the valley should be him now.

He takes the binoculars away from his eyes and carefully seals them back in their case. After another sip of water, he pushes himself back to his feet and on down the side of the valley towards the rendezvous. The sun will dip behind the hills soon. If he picks up his pace, he should be able to meet his guide before then; he doesn't like the idea of staggering around amongst the thorns and snakes in the dark, but equally, the FAQs suggest not to use a torch while attempting a night-time border penetration. If the sky remains clear, there might be enough moonlight for his Spex to brighten things up. His new, latest generation Companion and Spex are luxuries bought with proceeds from the liquidation windfall. They are loaded with grey-ware and are currently set to flight mode—all radios passively listening. From the air, or space, he could be a farmer checking his pistachio trees, or a herder following errant goats. A constant stream of encrypted traffic from all the nasty software running on the customised Mesh-sourced OSs he had installed before setting off would not be in character.

***

Once they are within shouting distance, his guide—if that's who it really is—waves. Anosh waves back and crosses the remaining scrub, joining the man beneath a massive olive tree. The overhanging bows and the thicket of leaves effectively hide them from the sky. They shake hands and the man, Ali, offers Anosh a glass of tea from a small aluminium pot he has boiling away over a smokeless fire of dry branches.

"Won't they see the fire?" Anosh asks.

"Farmers make fire. Everybody drinks tea."

Anosh nods and stirs in a spoonful of sugar, ignoring the black specks which are probably just ants. Ali even has biscuits and water; obviously he cares about his ratings.

A strategy that seems to pay off. Anosh had chosen him, although he charged more than most of the competition.

This is the Middle East; it isn't form to talk business before the first three glasses of tea have been drunk. So Anosh enjoys the refreshments and tries to make polite small talk.

"Will the moon be bright tonight?"

"No worry, moon rise late. We go early."

"Oh, good. We are going to cross before the moon comes up?"

"We go across when guards change, when sun go down."

"You have a good reputation, lots of happy customers, I guess?"

Ali puffs up. "I am best," he answers. "You like another biscuit?"

"Sure, thanks." Anosh accepts the yellow crumbly disk, then puts his hand in his pocket and takes out the little 1/10 ounce of Krugerrand—three grams of gold, half of the agreed price—and offers it to his guide.

Ali accepts it without a word and, after a minimum of inspection, it disappears inside his shirt. He hands back a deflated rubber balloon with a battery and an LED stuck to one end.

"Half now half later, okay?"

"Sure." Anosh knows the deal. 'Don't pay the ferry man' is the slogan on Ali's site.

"When you are on other side, put coin in balloon and toss back. Okay?"

Anosh inspects the little widget and then tucks it away into the pocket on the top of his rucksack. The sugary tea and water do him the world of good. By the time the sun is dipping between the distant mountains, shining its orange rays against the bottom of the feathery clouds, he is ready for action. If anything, the journey is an anti-climax. They quickly cross the three kilometres of scrub to the former Syrian border, a few poles linked by rusty tatters of wire mesh. Ali doesn't even slow down as they leave Kurdistan behind. Fifty metres of no-man's land, then there is a line of cleared vegetation stretching off in both directions with a more imposing, shiny new fence topped with razor wire running through the middle of it. A little winding path runs at an angle to the fence and then pushes under it through a furrow.

"Wait." Ali takes a plastic contraption out of his pack. It's about the size of a children's beach bucket with the bottom knocked out. It is threaded through with thousands of turns of thin wire. Something like an old set-top TV aerial pokes out of the middle. "Pigs make hole under fence, soldiers watch with camera."

They are waiting about ten metres away from the fence and crouch there behind a large spiky bush. Ali points towards a camera set on a pole on the Osmanian side. He sets up the device and points the aerial at it; then, flipping a little metal switch, it starts to whine.

"EMP?" Anosh asks.

Ali nods. "Go now, quick!"

Anosh races forward in a crouch and squeezes himself under; it's a tight fit and he has to take off his pack and push it before him as he wriggles through the scraping, where the wild pigs have made their run.

"Go hide in bush. Quick."

Anosh does as he is told and, as soon as he is out of sight of the camera, Ali fiddles with his device, and presumably somewhere a monitor is again showing a clear view of the fence. Probably the ten seconds of static will not be enough to justify sending out a jeep. Anosh should be long gone by then, anyway. As agreed, he takes the second Kruger from his pocket and pokes it into the little red balloon which Ali gave him. He switches on the tiny flashing LED duct-taped to its side and flings it all over the fence. The red LED traces out a broken arc in the dusk and Ali has no problems finding it and scooping up the flashing bundle from where it lands.

"Thanks!" Anosh shouts.

"No worries man," Ali replies in his strange hodge-podge accent. "Give good rating!"

"Will do! Five stars. Bye!"

Anosh takes out his Companion and checks the bearing to where his family should be waiting. Once he has put a few kilometres between himself and the border, he will connect to whatever networks he can find and see if there are any messages for him, but first he needs to do some serious walking.

Bad things had continued not to happen and Anosh was starting to take the proverbial smooth sailing for granted.

The twelve days on the decaying fishing boat, with a profitable side line in refugee smuggling, could have ended badly—mugged and murdered and tipped into the sea being Anosh's favourite night terror—but the crew, a mixed bunch of Greeks and Palestinians, had turned out to be friendly. As the days had slipped by, he had eventually relaxed enough to let his guard down; enjoying the conversations on deck in the evenings while sharing bottles of ouzo. Again, at Latakia, he had been paranoid, expecting that the Caliphate's Mutaween would be waiting for an infidel with a pack stuffed full of gold coins and subversive tech. He had fully expected to be arrested as a spy then. The FAQs were pretty clear about how bad an outcome that would be.

Now with Latakia behind him, he is enjoying the grey moonlit landscape as he walks casually amongst the olives and pistachios. He is thinking of being reunited with his family and, as it turns out, counting his chickens far too early.

There must be water nearby, as a chorus of frogs starts an electronica party. The hundreds of break-beat DJs chirping frantically somehow manage to merge into an ambient blanket of sound. Fragrances insinuate themselves into his sensorium, lulling his soul and drawing him out, smearing his existence, merging his awareness with the night.

The thump of a chopper takes a while to register. He isn't out for a Sunday stroll. He is suspiciously close to a militarised border, with no papers and a pack stuffed full of incriminating contraband. Eventually, his brain catches up and he drops to the dirt in the darkness. He wriggles his body into a thick bush that is growing around the trunk of another massive olive tree. A camouflaged infrared blanket is stashed at the top of his pack, ready in anticipation of exactly this scenario. He can feel his heart thudding as he fishes it out and drapes it over his head like a disco hijab.

There seem to be at least two of the big antique Russ helicopters. They are flying as a pair in formation, high-powered lights scanning the scrub for immigrants or terrorists. It would be too optimistic to hope the sensory suites on the choppers also date from the 1970s. Ironically, his Spex are flashing a yellow network icon that tells him that they are confident that they can send data, piggy-backing on the Mil-Net, out to the Mesh. It could be a trap, though, tempting him to send his packets out like a flock of startled doves and so give himself away. At the moment, the choppers seem to be flying away from him. He nestles down against the trunk, the camo-blanket loose over his head, and waits for them to leave.

An hour later, they are still around. It is beginning to look more like a directed search than a random patrol. His thoughts return to the crew of the little boat. Had the friendship been genuine as they filled his cup with ouzo?

Nervousness steps up to fear. Anosh decides to risk breaking radio silence. He can't penetrate the Mil-Net on his own. The upgraded software on his slate estimates it would take 240,000 years to crack, but that shouldn't be a problem. Each state has its own eclectic assortment of hardware purchased from West and East as the politics of the twentieth and twenty-first centuries played out. Russ helicopters and Prussian tanks, British subs and Çin fighter jets, like the nations that manufactured them, each communicates with its own mutually incomprehensible languages and protocols. Most pragmatic commanders simply run a second, much less secure, network over the same radios to let all the kit talk together. Anosh can't read their coms or hack their systems, but he can probably sneak a couple of packets into the network soup and out onto the Mesh.

He gets his Companion to encrypt a tiny message, according to the emergency format they set up:

'I am here: [X,Y], Undetected, Hiding, Assist if possible.'

He keeps it small enough so that it fits into a single packet and lets it swim off with their 'do not reply flag' set. The coordinates are a decoy, shifted eighty kilometres to the East along the border. If the Osmani manage to intercept his package and crack the code, he will see the choppers dash away towards the decoy; but if they simply triangulate on the radio carrier wave, then the whoosh of an incoming missile will be his only warning. They don't budge, which is good.

While he can hear the thudding blades, he makes sure he remains motionless, with his feet and elbows tucked in carefully under the stripped and blotched Mylar blanket.

'Be the rock, warmed by the sun.'

It seems to be working, as nobody has shot at him or sent streams of abseiling troops to flush him out; but equally, the choppers don't seem to be in any hurry to go home. They circle like aggressive angels, blinding both the transient and aboriginal denizens of the night with their all-seeing beams.

A few kilometres away, his family waits in an ancient Land Rover. They'd arrived in the area two days before Anosh's planned crossing and, with rising excitement, had spent the time subtly scoping out the border.

While Anosh had been waiting in a shabby little pension, Zaki had been suffering heat and discomfort, using illicit scripts and packages to intercept and record the encrypted coms from outposts and occasional foot patrols. Sleeping in a little tent and sheltering under trees in the day, their first task had been to farm out the captured data to one of the mercenary BotNets.

Ayşe had established their cover as a small family camping out by a scenic bend on a dried-up stream. She spoke with the curious local kids, who passed by with their goats. While she was busy, the boys sank their senses into the sparse local Mesh, drawing together threads and favours to build some sort of defence in case Anosh's crossing didn't run as smoothly as they all hoped.

When Zaki was ten, Anosh had shown him how to code a simple 'run and jump' game and, since then, he has thought himself a hacker. Although, in reality, he is little more than script kiddie plankton on the hacker food chain, there is so much grey-ware on the Mesh that, over the past several months, with the curtains drawn and his twisted, aching back protesting, he has been ghosting on forums, reading rockstar hacker posts, downloading and configuring packages and, in a short time, educating himself to a government unsettling level of proficiency on electronic insurgency.

Segi, meanwhile, had been pulling in favours from their friends and trying to deal with the fickle, treacherous BotNets. These massive swarms of ad hoc semi-autonomous computation were constantly under attack from the governments and corporations they mocked, and pulled and stretched in all directions by hackers of all hat colours, who tried to co-opt their super powers. Most were parts of the greater Mesh; running as DACs, they charged for services, and paid their own rents. They were accountable only to their own opaque algorithmic morality. They lost data and gave up on jobs, without explanation. There were no money-back guarantees.

Cracking the DT08-q that the Osmani were using should have taken hours and a significant quantity of MeshCoins, but after the initial upload and Coin transfer had cleared, Segi only had to wait twenty seconds before the keys arrived on his Companion. Other parties were eavesdropping on the Osmanian border patrols today, and the BotNet had either cached the keys from an earlier job or bought them from a peer. They sent the keys through to Anosh, but he was already on his way, under a thick cloak of radio silence.

While Zaki had been using the keys to hack into the coms, Siegfried had prepared interference packages full of beautiful false starts and decoys if things turned bad. He had used his reputation and promises of contribution to a bunch of projects to draft help. His virtual team had been creating realistic-sounding reports and even low-quality video of civilian bodies lying in pools of blood. It was trivial stuff when given anything more than a cursory glance, but hopefully it would do some good if they needed it.

Zaki is lying stretched out on the tatty backseat of the Land Rover, when he suddenly knows his father is in trouble. Spex worked like that. He hadn't read the message, hadn't even noticed, as it blitted itself across his visual field, just as he didn't notice his own blind spot. Meaning passed into his brain by osmosis, subconsciously extracted and incorporated into the set of things he knew. His brother and mother are only sitting a metre away, but it is easier to IM them than to spend time talking. He forwards the contents of the coded packet Anosh had sent, adding the location of the two helicopters.

A few seconds later, their mother finishes reading the alert and starts panicking and begins to ask obvious questions; however, by then, the boys are already well into their choreographed response.

Segi's first interference package looks like a transcript of PKF coms, intercepted from a foot patrol. It places a raiding force at the fake coordinates of their dad's distress message. Zaki, fingers flashing expertly on the Companion's small screen, runs the script that will use today's BotNet sourced certificates to inject Segi's distraction into the Osmanian Mil-Net. Once dispatched, the boys hold their breath.

Two and a half minutes later, out on the horizon, one of the choppers stops its sedate patrolling, then turns and thunders off. Zaki exhales with relief and, a few minutes later, uploads the second package: a report from a small village police station twenty kilometres deeper into Osmaniye—an explosion has been heard and there is shooting, possibly injured civilians. Siegfried attaches the faked video to the report. Another minute later and the boys whoop and high five as the second helicopter goes chasing off after the mirage of a major PKF operation.

Anosh watches from under his blanket, with a mixture of relief, pride and disbelief as the helicopters leave. As soon as it is safe, he crumples the blanket back into his pack. With stiff legs from hours of sitting motionless he begins to hobble, then jog, though the night. He is following the hovering green arrow that his Spex are creating, vague fears of snakes forgotten against the very real threat of death from above. His Spex manage to highlight some of the stones or branches, but more than once he picks himself up, cursing a stubbed toe or a bruised shin.

While the helicopters are following ghosts beyond the hills, the barrage of industrial noise is gone. It is peaceful and, although chaos whirls around him, here, jogging through the eye of the storm, it is calm.

As he runs, Anosh steps back along the chain of trust that transported him across Europe. He doesn't want to think the faces that now march across the stage of his mind have betrayed him, but with resignation and without malice, he accepts that at least one of them probably has.

Economics is trust. A breach of trust bleeds reputation from the system. It is a zero sum game and, although the negative impact will percolate back in the form of bad ratings or lost points, his betrayer must have calculated that exchanging trust for wealth was a rational course of action: wealth will flow to him, while negative impact will be spread along the web of trust.

A strident rising sequence of cracking percussions reintroduces the hunter's song to the orchestra of the night. The sound is carried on the wind, echoing between land and the thermoclines of cooling night air, lensing and surging, a dread beating.

Perhaps it was the junior prison guard, who had smuggled him into port, or one of the riggers on the boat to Latakia. It doesn't make him angry; it doesn't even make him sad. It is just disappointing.

He finds himself crying, then, picturing his family so close, waiting for him to scrabble out of the scrub and into their arms.

A row of bushes appears ahead; it marks the edge of a dirt road. A pair of faint lights flicker into existence over the crest of a low hill. Shining into the dusty night, the beams are visible only intermittently as they flash skyward.

He can hear the copters getting closer. He squats back from the road next to a large, wedge-shaped boulder. He pulls the camouflaged Mylar thermal blanket back over himself and waits. The material crinkles and rustles. It becomes clammy with his condensed breath and sweat. As the helicopters move overhead, the car, a battered-looking Land Rover, dashes by. It's too dark and dusty to get a view of the occupants, so he stays hunkered down and invisible beneath his camouflage.

***

The helicopters are back again. Ayşe is driving with her scarf pulled across her face to keep out the dust. The windows are open. Anosh should be around here somewhere, and they don't want to miss him. Segi is on the back seat. From under a blanket, he is listening hard to pick up any chatter from the radios. From the scraps they can intercept, it's not looking good. The Osmani know there is at least one person trying to sneak across their border tonight.

Zaki is sitting in the passenger seat, scanning the scrub on either side of the road. A jeep is approaching, still a couple of kilometres away, but visible from its headlights as it crawls along another dirt track on the opposite side of the shallow valley.

The closest helicopter, about five hundred metres away behind them, is dropping down and lifting a thick boiling plume of dust, backlit by the lights of the approaching jeep. Ayşe eases off the accelerator and lets the rough terrain slow them down.

Zaki watches something detach from the helicopter. A few moments later, he sees the unmistakable silhouettes of bodies abseiling down lines and dropping into the seething maelstrom of dust.

***

Anosh had known the game was up when the choppers returned. They criss-crossed the night in a deliberate patient grid. They seemed to know he was somewhere below, and they weren't going anywhere. He had followed advice and physically turned off all his kit and now sat huddled, motionless, under his Mylar blanket.

Suddenly, his Spex ear buds crackle. He pulls them out of his ears to double check they are off. They crackle again, and this time there is a simultaneous thread of pain that pulses briefly at his temple and inside his head.

The other helicopter swings around, orienting itself towards him like a hunting thing. He feels like a rabbit in the long grass, crouching motionless while the lynx approaches, its ears swivelling first as it picks up some tiny betraying sound, then its head follows to bring its awful gaze and deadly intent to bare.

He knows they have found him, pulsed him with enough EM radiation that all the wires and aerials in his equipment resonate in sympathy, sending back faint involuntary responses, modulated with identifying and incriminating information proclaiming him as not goat-herder.

It is practically above him now. At this range, they can probably detect his heartbeat with their Doppler radar, despite his vest sown through with metal threads. The air is full of dust, and it is appallingly loud. Through the orange confusion, a bundle of rope drops into a clear area between the olive trees. It starts to jerk and then the dark form of a body appears through the dust, only about twenty metres away from where he is hiding.

He can barely breathe with all the dust and the mind-numbing waves of pressure that wash in from the helicopter's rotors. He is trapped between the thick trunk of an ancient olive and a large boulder. More shapes are moving between the trees; they are black and menacing and cast long, sharp shadows with distorted arms which grope out through the orange, translucent air. He can hear the crackle of radios. Blinding lights strobe across the now alien countryside. Suddenly he is blind. The sharp shadows of the bush he is crouched inside become skeletal fingers against the light. The black shapes have all turned in his direction now and are approaching.

The rabbit bolts, fight or flight. Standing up, letting the camouflage blanket get ripped off by branches, he is incapable of conscious thought. He stumbles through the bushes, away from the lights. A small voice is trying to insist they have found him, despite everything, and one man stumbling in the dark is not going to give them the slip; but the voice is submerged by panic and sensory overload.

***

Two flashes are followed by loud muted cracks, light and sound dissociated through distance. Somebody in the car screams. Ayşe stops with a skid that throws up another thick ball of dust. As it rises and floats forward, it temporarily masks everything outside its perimeter. The dread within the car settles. Nobody speaks. They are all looking off, through the dusty soup, towards the still-hovering helicopter. The jeep is much closer, but has also stopped a few hundred metres away around a bend.

After two or three minutes, shapes begin to appear on the ropes again. This time, they ascend, one after another, smoothly sliding up into the belly of the hunter. There is another pause, and then a last silhouette ascends. As soon as the last shape is inside, the helicopter begins to climb and bank away from them.

Zaki is pretty sure that none of the shapes he watched entering the helicopter were his father. Ascending a rope, into a hovering helicopter, even with some form of powered climbing assist, is not a skill he could imagine Anosh secretly acquiring.

The jeep in front is coming around the corner now. The helicopter has risen another ten metres.

Perhaps, it was a false alarm. Perhaps, the soldiers shot and missed. Or perhaps, Anosh is lying out there somewhere, bleeding into the stony earth.

Zaki watches the rope swinging slowly, like a pendulum below the wasp shape of the rising black copter. There is something hanging from its end.

The jeep is black. It has lights on its roof. They are flashing. It pulls up next to them, rolling slowly to a halt. Its driver is obviously familiar with the local conditions and keen to avoid adding to the excessive amount of dust already suspended in the air.

Ayşe and Segi are watching it as it draws level with them. Zaki is still intent on the departing evil. The rope is disappearing back into its body. It is now a winged spider drawing in its lines. A limp, wrapped shape is tangled in the final length of web.

As the helicopter swings around to a new heading, the bundle on the end, the weight on the pendulum, traces a lazy arc in the sky, a segment of circumference. Neither Ayşe nor Siegfried have noticed.

The policeman has wound down his window, and he is shouting something to Ayşe above the noise. Zaki is calm. With a few discreet taps, his Companion translates the sounds, printing words on its screen and whispering to him through his ear buds.

"What are you doing here?" it translates.

Ayşe is staring at the policeman, terrified, frozen.

"What are you doing here?" the cop repeats the sounds again.

Zaki leans over awkwardly and answers, parroting the words his earbuds speak into his ear: "Going home."

The policeman looks past the insensitive Ayşe to Zaki, craning over from the passenger seat.

"What's wrong with your mother?" the cop asks, taking in Zaki's twisted hand and contorted posture.

Zaki's other hand is hidden by his mother's body. He types his response and then repeats aloud his Companion's translation, hoping he is making some kind of sense in Turkic, hoping the policeman will assume they are just a family of imbeciles and cripples.

"She's deaf."

The policeman scans the interior of the car, mentally fitting the occupants to his preconceptions of a family unit. "Where is your father?"

The doll, tiny and far away now, is fastened at the waist and hangs face up. Its arms and legs are splayed awkwardly. It swings and turns in the wind as it dangles below the departing chopper.

Zaki types words and then repeats sounds that have no meaning.

"Our father is dead."

END OF BOOK ONE

CLV2 is lying in the sun waiting amongst the sand and scrub.

```
No bogies detected.
Situation nominal.
No orders in queue.
```

Time passes.

```
Unfriendly units approaching.
```

CLV2 stirs, jacks ver chassis into drive mode and tracks the coordinates.

'So there are,' ve thinks to verself. 'Where did they come from?'

Two Main Battle Tanks are thundering across the dunes towards ver. Range 1800M.

The nuclear fire at CLV2's heart swells and power surges into ultra-capacitors and momentum stores.

Ve simulates the situation for a few milliseconds then fires two shots from each of the large coil gun barrels on ver main turret. HEAP rounds arc away on ballistic trajectories, on target...
...but the rounds never make contact, detonating instead a few metres out, dousing the two enemy tanks with nothing more substantial than clouds of smoke.

```
Security compromised.
```

CLV2 checks the magazine; the rounds are correctly signed.

The certificates all check out as High Explosive Armour Piercing. Yet, empirical observation contradicts this received knowledge.

```
Error.
Data consistency compromised.
Probable result of hostile electronic warfare attack.
```

CLV2 performs a scan of the area. 200m West is a glass wall; sitting behind it on tiers of wooden benches are a group of humans holding optical devices and mobile communication gear. They are not assisting ver, nor displaying any of the usual human physiological fear or panic indicators.

CLV2, confused and under attack, incorrectly concludes that they must be part of the enemy deployment.

How did they penetrate so far inside the homeland battle space?
CLV2 fires a fusillade of shells from ver 30mm cannon towards the stands. Ver microwave radar cannot find the departing rounds and ve quickly shuts off the guns. Blanks, more electronic warfare corruption!

Ve is hobbled, compromised. CLV2 is classified 'Top Secret' and knows it. High priority standing orders compel ver to prevent the intelligence within ver systems from falling into enemy hands. CLV2 begins to feel the self-destruct itch.

Ve scans the humans again. They are certainly going to rake through the debris for intelligence once the tanks close and finish ver off.

CLV2 goes into simulation mode again, branching and pruning vast trees of possibilities; once the optimal course of action presents itself ve doesn't hesitate. Targeting lasers pushed to maximum power lance out and slash across the faces of the watching humans. Spex and eyeballs blacken or burst like popcorn. Before the humans have had time to start screaming, ve runs the lasers back, targeting all hands holding communication devices; Companions clatter to the floor and the air is filled with screams and the smell of roasting pork. Having hopefully bought verself some time, ve starts accelerating towards the closing tanks.

There are a further 37 seconds of peace before the enemy starts firing. CLV2 cannot account for this pause; ve doesn't have time to crack the coms, so cannot hear the frenzied conversations between the tank pilots and the HQ. Ve doesn't know that live go-codes must be hastily requested and approved, cannot see the closing tanks ejecting blank rounds and replacing them with live munitions.

The autonomous point defence laser turrets start illuminating incoming shells, managing to detonate or deflect a few in mid-flight, but the shells are coming in thick and fast, and some inevitably get through.

CLV2 calls for support. There is one bird within range, a surveillance drone with its optics pointed towards the action. Despite repeated pings and valid identity tokens, it will not accept CLV2's go-codes. The electronic warfare infiltration must have scrambled those, too. Ve cannot persuade the drone to attack the tanks with its admittedly puny weapon systems. After a logical dance ending in some nasty buffer overflows and compromised sandboxes, CLV2's superior intellect eventually triumphs. The drone reluctantly accepts a new heading.

Half ver drive wheels are non-functioning. Large sections of armour and interior are missing or on fire. There is major damage to the reactor shielding. It needs a constant act of will now to suppress the self-destruct urge.

The nearest tank is only fifty metres away. The other is coming round to fire again and ve notices that the crew hatch is still open. Ve sends off an updated course to the drone and watches as it adjusts its heading.

Ve faints to the left then swings sharply to the right, breaking with ver front wheels and dropping the front suspension as much as possible. With a final burst of acceleration, the wedge-like front of CLV2's armour smashes into the ground and grinds under the enemy tank, ploughing towards it. CLV2 detonates the explosive bolts on ver forward maintenance hatch, which is now pointing up under the belly of the flailing enemy tank. The hatch flies up, doing very minor damage to the underside of the tank seesawing backwards and forwards on CLV2's forward section.

One last time, CLV2 scans the surrounding area; everything is consistent with ver planning simulation: the tank wedged up on ver front section will not be able to free itself for several seconds; the 2nd tank, roaring in at top speed, will be able to fire again in 700 ms; the drone, grumbling with proximity and collision alerts, is approaching fast and will arrive shortly after CLV2 ceases to be.

With something like relief, ve finally triggers ver self-destruct charges.

An exploding ball of super-heated gas wallops through CLV2's interior spaces, purging and deleting. The explosion drives itself in a 60cm wide column out of the hole where the inspection hatch used to be. Like a rocket-powered plasma cutter, it punches through the vulnerable under armour of the tank above and fire rages through this second enclosed space, cleaning and killing.

Three seconds later and 800m away, back at the chaos of the viewing benches, the few guests who are still conscious are able to witness a flash screaming in from above. The drone, obeying its last orders, slams down at 600mph through the open hatch of the second tank and explodes spectacularly inside.

Note from the Author:

I hope you are enjoying the story so far.
As an indie author I depend on reviews from readers
like you to get the word out!

If you've enjoyed this book, please consider
rating and reviewing it.

www.Amazon.com

For news, updates and freebies,
you can subscribe to my newsletter:
www.tobyweston.net

More Singularity's Children...

Book Two, Disruption

Book Three, Conflict

Printed in Great Britain
by Amazon